Your Friendly
Neighbourhood
Death Pedlar

Your Friendly Neighbourhood Death Pedlar

JIMMY SANGSTER

DODD, MEAD & COMPANY • NEW YORK

First published in the United States 1972

ISBN: 0-396-06508-2
Library of Congress Catalog Card Number: 77-184188
Printed in the United States of America
by The Haddon Craftsmen, Inc., Scranton, Penna.

To

CAROLYN

1

THE QUESTIONNAIRE WAS BRIEF AND IMPERSONAL. Nevertheless, it took Anthony a good fifteen minutes to fill it in. He had always found it difficult to describe himself accurately; it was a difficulty tinged with embarrassment. He had long ago decided that it was because there was so little to describe. If the questionnaire had asked him to describe what he looked like, he would have written down height, average; hair, fairish; eyes, bluish; teeth, goodish; face, ordinary; build, medium. If it had asked him what he did best, and he had been feeling honest with himself, he would have written down "not much of anything". And if asked to enlarge on this he would have been forced to admit that he didn't hold a very

9

high opinion of himself; he was basically shy, and only wanted to be left alone to bumble through life in his own good time, doing his own thing. He wasn't quite sure yet what his thing was, but he was confident that it would turn up one day and he would recognise it when it did. But the questionnaire didn't probe that deeply, so he was spared the uncomfortable experience of self-analysis which bugged him occasionally.

NAME:	*Anthony John Bridges*
ADDRESS:	*14 Carlton Place Mews,*
	London S.W.1.
	England.
AGE:	*29.*
SEX:	*Male.*
MARITAL STATUS:	*Single.*
NATIONALITY:	*British.*
FATHER'S NATIONALITY:	*British.*
MOTHER'S NATIONALITY:	*British.*
FATHER'S PROFESSION:	*Minister of the Church*
EDUCATION:	
Public School:	*Boxed.*
University:	*Leeds.*
Degrees:	*Bachelor of Arts.*
EMPLOYMENT RECORD:	*Three years in the Army after leaving University. Short-service commission (Second Lieutenant). One year copywriting for Advertising agency. Two years with BBC TV on documentary films.*

*Two years with the Lem-
stock Corporation as Sales
Representative.
At present unemployed.*

OTHER INFORMATION: *None.*

Anthony read it over. It didn't look very impressive. Perhaps he should have bent the truth a little. After all, some things would be difficult to check up on; the chances of being caught out in a lie were minimal. He crossed out Bachelor of Arts and substituted Master of Arts. What if they wanted to know the reason why he had left the Lemstock Corporation? That was something they *could* check up on; and remembering those bastards who had given him the sack, and their perfectly valid reasons for doing so, the less anyone knew of that affair, the better. Better cross out Lemstock altogether. But that left a two year gap in his Employment Record. Put down "self employed" and hope they didn't ask at what. "At present unemployed" didn't look too good either. He crossed that out as well and wrote instead "at present taking a sabbatical". Then, in case he hadn't spelled it correctly, he looked it up in his paperback dictionary.

SABBATICAL: of or like the Sabbath. *Bible:* every seventh year when the earth lies fallow.

That covered it, he thought. I'm lying just about as fallow as is humanly possible. He read through the questionnaire once more. It looked much better, he decided. Using a pen this time, he inked over what he had written in pencil. Then he waited for the ink to dry before rubbing out the pencil with a soft eraser. He blew off the scraps of eraser from the questionnaire, folded it neatly, and put it in an envelope which he had already stamped and addressed.

*　　　　*　　　　*

Lilian was in the sitting room, her feet up, watching the Sunday afternoon movie on the television. "I'm going down to the post box," he said. She didn't even acknowledge his existence. He considered for a moment whether there would be any gain in hitting her over the head with the table lamp; then he thought, the hell with it. After all, it was her apartment; she paid the rent and bought the food; at least, Daddy did, which amounted to the same thing. And anyway, she wasn't a bad bird as birds go. A bit demanding in bed, but that was the reason she had put up with him at the beginning. Running to a little fat these last few weeks, but still reasonably attractive by most standards. The day that he had run across her had been like Christmas and his birthday rolled into one. Both bored at a party, they had found themselves alone in one corner of the room. All around was alcoholically induced freneticism. She looked too pretty to ignore, so he had introduced himself. They had talked inconsequentials for half an hour, then by mutual consent they had left the party together, both deserting the dates they had arrived with. They had moved on to a drinking club in the King's Road, where they had become slowly blasted. Round about two in the morning, Anthony suddenly remembered something.

"I've got nowhere to sleep tonight," he said.

"Why not?"

"I've been sharing with this fellow. We had a sort of row."

"What sort of a row?"

12

"Seems he's a faggot and I never knew it until he started to come on strong last night."

"Bit late to start thinking of finding a bed, isn't it?" said Lilian.

"I was going to stop over at Jane's. She's the bird I came to the party with. Can't very well do that now."

"You sleeping with her on a regular sort of basis?" asked Lilian.

"I'm not sleeping with her at all as a matter of fact," replied Anthony. "She's got a spare bed."

Lilian stared into her drink for a long moment, then looked up at him from her smoky blue eyes. "I've got a spare bed," she said.

"Ta," said Anthony; and that was that.

He had been there three months now and he had never gone anywhere near the spare bed. Not that he didn't earn his room and board, he thought, as he slammed the front door and started up the street towards the post box. Who'd have thought a little bird like Lilian, what with her upper echelon upbringing, Roedean and Switzerland, could turn out to be such a raving maniac beneath the sheets? He grinned to himself at the expression "beneath the sheets". On the floor; on the table; in the armchair; across the back of the settee; on the stairs; on the bannisters; in the bath; in the car; in the park; in the swimming pool; in the cinema, the theatre, the train; the afternoon, the evening, the morning; over breakfast, tea and dinner. In three months of what seemed in retrospect to have been one long fornication, he couldn't remember once having done it "beneath the sheets". And by Christ, he was tired. Not that he didn't enjoy sex, because he did. No, he was tired of being part of the furnishings in Lilian's well ordered existence. She had a kitchen to use when she was hungry; she had a bedroom to use when she was tired; and she had Anthony to use when she was randy.

And recently he had started to realise that she wouldn't be at all averse to making the arrangement permanent. For the first couple of months she had kept him well hidden from her friends in general and Mummy and Daddy in particular. Then she had started taking him out places. And, two weeks ago, had come the "weekend". In spite of the warmth of the Sunday afternoon sun, Anthony shivered slightly when he recalled the "weekend". It had come as a complete surprise to him when she nudged him awake that Saturday morning.

"Come on," she'd said. "Musn't be late."

"For what?" As far as he was concerned, Saturday was "pub-crawl-down-the-King's-Road" day, and that didn't start until eleven-thirty a.m. at the earliest.

"We're going down to the cunt," said Lilian, who liked to cut the last syllable off a word occasionally, especially when the result could be misconstrued.

"Where in the country?" asked Anthony, who had absolutely no desire to go anywhere except the *Chelsea Potter* in two hours' time.

"We're spending the weekend with Mummy and Daddy," she said.

Then she bounded out of bed and locked herself in the bathroom before Anthony could think of anything to say. It seemed the time had come when he was to be presented to the parents. These same parents that Lilian had taken such pains to hide him from to date. Indeed, on more than one occasion, he had been forced to pack his things, hide his toothbrush and razor and move out of the house at one hour's notice; all because "Mummy was up for some shop-

14

ping and was dropping in for tea". The forthcoming confrontation could only mean one thing as far as Anthony could see; Lilian was proposing to make an honest man out of him.

He dressed sulkily, and he was still sulking half an hour later when they climbed into Lilian's car. He didn't argue when she got into the driving seat as he usually did, and he hardly spoke more than two words to her for the first hour. Then what with the top of the car being down, and the sun shining, and the radio playing, and the hangover dissolving, he had decided that he would try to make an effort towards being gracious.

"Tell me about your mother and father," he said.

She answered him without taking her eyes from the road. "What's to tell. They're my parents."

"What are they like?"

"Rich."

"I know that, but what are they like?"

She shrugged. "Like parents," she said.

Not like mine, thought Anthony, with a barely repressed shudder. Anthony's father was a country vicar, a man totally lacking in any of the vices or virtues of a normal human being. The Reverend Jonathon Bridges existed solely to Spread the Word, which he did with a complete disregard of whether anyone heard it or not. His wife, Anthony's mother, was a small, insignificant little body, living totally in the almost non-existent shadow created by her husband; indeed, she was so insignificant that Anthony had trouble recalling what she looked like ten minutes after one of his infrequent filial visits. No, Lilian's parents couldn't be anything like his, he decided.

"Do they know about me?" he asked.

"They know I've got a boy-friend. But not that we co-habitate. Not on any permanent basis anyway."

"They know we've slept together though?"

"I don't suppose they've given it much thought."

"I mean like they don't imagine you're a virgin or anything like that?"

She glanced at him, taking her eyes off the road for an instant. She smiled briefly and Anthony decided that this was one of her prettier days. "I'm twenty-four," she said. "Even here in the wilds of deepest Surrey, there's no such creature as a twenty-four-year-old virgin. They're an extinct species, my love."

Anthony allowed a few moments to elapse before getting on to the subject he considered important. Then he cleared his throat awkwardly, a habit he had whenever he wasn't quite sure how what he was about to say was going to be received. "Is there any particular object to this exercise?" he asked.

"Like what?" she said, unhelpfully.

"Like I mean, why are you suddenly offering me up for parental inspection?"

"Don't you want to meet them?" she said, ominously.

"Certainly," he said. "Dying to."

"Stop complaining then."

"I'm not complaining; I'm just curious."

She jammed the brakes on suddenly, nearly pitching him over the windscreen and earning herself an agonised hoot of protest from the car behind her. She pulled into a layby, switched off the engine, and then, with her hands still on the steering wheel, she turned to face him.

'You start getting grotty with me, darling, and I'll cut your balls off," she said.

"I'm not getting grotty," said Anthony, who was more

16

surprised than anything else. "I'm just asking a simple question. Why am I being dragged off to meet the heretonow mythical Mummy and Daddy? I just want to know, that's all."

She stared hard at him for a couple of seconds and suddenly Anthony practically recoiled in horror; her eyes had gone watery, she was on the point of crying, he realised. He put a hand out to touch her, but she dragged herself away from physical contact.

"You're such a shit," she said. "A big, big shit."

Anthony was flabbergasted. "What have I *done*?" he asked.

"All you want to do is fuck," she said. "That's all I am to you, a permanent lay."

"I thought . . ."

She didn't let him finish. "No you didn't. You never do. And that's because you think with your cock. You're . . . you're an animal."

Anthony thought of the nights he had longed for sleep while she had been swarming all over him; but it didn't seem a good time to bring it up. "You never said anything," he said, lamely.

"Girls aren't supposed to," she said. "It's up to the man to make the first move."

Oh God, thought Anthony, it's love! Here we go with the hearts and flowers and the violins and cherry blossoms and the till death do us part. He felt a sinking feeling in his stomach, not unlike the hangover that he had recently got rid of. It wasn't that he was unromantic; in fact he was the opposite; for as long as he could remember he had nursed a half-formed dream involving an elegant, beautiful, talented woman whose voice was like melting honey and whose lips were like pale velvet. This woman loved him to distraction, and was adored

17

by him in return. In his dreams they would spend long hours together gazing into each other's eyes, holding hands and making soft, gentle love. They would never be out of each other's sight; they would never want to be; their entire lives would be complete within one another. Until this woman came along Anthony was prepared to fall half in and half out of love as many times as the opportunity presented itself. This was the case with Lilian, because she sure as hell wasn't the divine creature of his dreams. And now he wondered how he was going to tell her without hurting her too badly. Because he *was* fond of her, and he hated to hurt *anyone*. He tried to think of something to say that would let her down easily. This time when he reached out to take her hand, she allowed it.

"I'm sorry, darling," he said. "You know how I feel about you."

"Tell me," she said, unmollified.

"I didn't think I had to."

"You have to,' she countered, starting to drag her hand free.

He recaptured it quickly, not wanting to break the contact. "As much as I am capable of loving anyone, I love you," he said. He tried to put a great deal of feeling into his voice; he wanted to sound like a man who was nursing a great hurt somewhere in his past, something that he hadn't been able to talk about before because it was just too, too painful. And he must have halfway succeeded. She looked at him steadily for a moment, then she returned the pressure of his hand.

"Oh, darling," she said. "Darling, darling, darling!" And suddenly she was all over him, her arms wrapped round his neck, her mouth chewing at his. He allowed this for a moment, then he started to push her away gently.

18

"Not here, darling," he said. She looked up from where she had been undoing his zip.

"Why not here?"

He nodded out of the front of the car. There was a family saloon parked a few yards farther down the layby, and the occupants, including the three children, were sitting beside their car, surrounded by picnic litter, all staring at Anthony and Lilian with unabashed fascination. Reluctantly Lilian slid back into the driving seat, allowing Anthony to zip himself up. The crisis was over for the time being, thought Anthony. Later, he would have to explain more fully what he had meant, but that was later. Meanwhile, he had the weekend to get through.

*　　　*　　　*

Somehow, over the months he had known Lilian, Anthony had built up a mental picture of Mummy and Daddy. Mummy was slim, elegant and dressed in chiffon and picture hats; she presided at garden parties, opened fetes, and was terribly involved in "good works". Daddy was ex-military, tall and quietly impressive; he was Master of Hounds and a gentleman farmer; he travelled up to the City no more than three times each week where, from a sombrely beautiful, book-lined, leather-laden office, he ruled his financial empire; a Merchant Banker to rival the Rothschilds. They were the backbone of England, were Mummy and Daddy, never out of Jennifer's Diary and well in line for Birthday Honours any day now. So, wanting to impress even if only for Lilian's sake, Anthony sharpened up his county accent and prepared to bemoan the loss of the Empire.

*　　　*　　　*

19

The house was pretty impressive; hideous, but impressive nevertheless. Architecturally it defied classification. It took Anthony thirty seconds to decide that it was Elizabethan-Georgian-Victorian with a smattering of Frank Lloyd Wright thrown in for good measure. "Early ugly," Anthony christened it. It was approached up a long drive that meandered between immaculate lawns, scattered with flowering rhododendron bushes. Perched as it was on the crest of a small rise, it was plainly visible from the main road, and the mind boggled at the speculation it must have caused among passing motorists. It was. Anthony realised, the single most hideous edifice he had ever clapped eyes on, not excluding the Albert Memorial. His mental image of Mummy and Daddy began to totter.

"What does your father do?" he asked, as the car swept up the drive.

"Mm? Oh, he buys things and sells things," said Lilian vaguely. Not a Merchant Banker then, thought Anthony. More a Prince of Commerce, a latter day Cecil Rhodes.

Lilian parked the car beside a Silver Shadow Rolls in front of the house and climbed out. Anthony climbed out too, only a couple of seconds later; the sheer ugliness of the house had a soporific effect on him and close up it was almost over-powering.

"What do you think of the house?" asked Lilian, taking his hand and starting up towards the front door.

"Impressive," said Anthony.

"I grew up here," said Lilian.

Poor little thing, thought Anthony.

The front door was opened by a butler, an immensely impressive individual, six feet tall and as fat as butter. He bowed briefly when he saw Lilian, his eyes flicking once lightly over Anthony.

20

"Welcome home, Miss Lilian," he said in a voice which could have earned him a fortune on television commercials.

"How are you, Benskin?" asked Lilian.

"Well, thank you, Miss. And I trust you are the same?"

"Surviving, Benskin, surviving. This is Mr. Bridges."

He bowed once more, not so deeply this time. Anthony started to stick out his hand, but Lilian was holding it, and she jerked it back to his side.

"Bags are in the car, Benskin. Where are Mummy and Daddy?"

"Madam is in the drawing room, Miss." He looked at Anthony again, his eyes gleaming. He knows, thought Anthony; he saw that I was going to commit a social gaffe and shake his hand and he hates me for it. So fuck him, decided Anthony. He wrested his hand free from Lilian's and stuck it out towards Benskin.

"How do you do, Benskin?" he said. The gleam went from the eye, and the edifice started to crumple. There was a moment's hesitation and then the butler placed his limp hand in Anthony's.

"How do you do, sir?" said Benskin sorrowfully.

"Why did you do that?" said Lilian, as Benskin went outside to fetch in the cases.

"I always shake butlers' hands," said Anthony. "It saves me having to tip them."

Lilian looked for a moment as though she would have liked to have said something else, then she changed her mind. "Come on," she said. She took his hand again and started across the hall towards a pair of doors at the far end. Anthony had the vague impression of a huge sweep of staircase, an immensely high ceiling topped with a stained glass dome, and marble underfoot; then Lilian was pushing open the double doors into the drawing room.

The drawing room was sixty feet long and thirty feet broad. It looked as though it had been furnished by Salvador Dali on one of his off days.

"Oh God," said Lilian as they came in. "She's changed it again."

"Let's come down next weekend instead," said Anthony. "With any luck she'll have changed it back again."

Lilian giggled. "You didn't see it before. This is an improvement." Then she spotted Mummy doing something to a man-eating plant across the far side of the room.

"Hello darling," she called.

Mummy turned towards the voice, and Anthony's last image crumbled. "Coo-eee, luv!" screeched Mummy, drawing herself up to her full five feet two inches.

He watched while Lilian and Mummy kissed and cuddled their welcomes. Then, as Lilian took Mummy's arm and started to lead her towards him, he pinned on a smile and stepped forward.

"Anthony, this is Mummy. Mummy, Anthony Bridges."

"How do you do?" said Anthony.

"Very well thank you," said Mummy. "How do *you* do?" She stuck out a podgy little hand and Anthony shook it. "Lil's told us such a lot about you," said Mummy. "Me and Dad have been waiting to meet you for ages."

That's news, thought Anthony.

"She's told me a lot about you, too," he lied. "I've been looking forward to it."

She looked up at him with a vague smile still in place, and Anthony noticed that her eyes were very cold. "I'm sure you have," she said. Then she took Lilian's arm and started to

22

lead her away, talking about what she was going to do with the drawing room as she was already a bit fed up with the Dali influence. Rather than just stand there, Anthony started to follow them.

"Where's Daddy?" he heard Lilian say.

"He's upstairs with his sexatary," said Mummy. Jesus Christ, thought Anthony, she can't even pronounce the simplest words correctly. As though divining his thoughts, Mummy suddenly turned back to him. "Wait until you see her, Anthony, luv. You'll get my meaning right enough." And, horror upon horror, she dug her elbow into his ribs and chuckled.

Anthony glanced at Lilian; surely she was putting him on; in a couple of minutes this old harridan would be sent below stairs where she belonged and Lilian would introduce Mummy proper; then they would all have a chuckle over dinner at the jolly old wheeze they had all played on Lilian's boy-friend. But, apart from looking a little drawn around the mouth, Lilian remained expressionless.

"Sit down Anthony," said Mummy, waving towards a chair. "Don't mind Lil and me. We've got family talking to catch up on."

Anthony sat down and tried to smile casually, as he half listened to what Mummy was telling Lilian. It wasn't interesting unless one had a personal stake in Dad's drinking and playing around, or in Mummy's arthritis. The other half of his mind surveyed the room and the furnishings. There was a grand piano painted scarlet, with one large eye inlaid with mother-of-pearl staring from the centre of the raised lid; standing against the wall was the life sized stone form of a naked man. The statue had been decapitated and a sunburst clock placed where the head had been. A piece of brightly coloured gauze had been draped over the crotch and one of the outstretched hands clutched a bunch of carnations. The chair that Anthony was sitting in had arms carved in the shape of female human legs and if he lay his own arms along the arms of the chair, he found that he was clutching on to the feet. He glanced down between his legs; sure enough, the legs of the chair were carved like the arms and hands of a woman, the palms resting flat on the floor. There was a standard lamp which looked like a giant grey phallus, but which on closer inspection turned out to be an elephant's trunk wired down the centre to keep it rigid. There was a life sized statue of a beautiful female body with a large fresh cabbage where the head should be; there was a gazebo taking up the entire far wall, stuffed with the most outrageously opulent flowers and plants Anthony had ever even dreamed of. There was a stuffed tiger with an ornately studded Mexican saddle thrown over its back; and there was Mummy herself. Anthony found himself regarding her surreptitiously as she rabitted on to Lilian. She was about fifty-five and she had the sort of face that Anthony could only describe as "weather beaten". She was wearing a disastrously patterned dress that looked as though it had been cut on her with a knife and fork. The dress reached below her knees, for which Anthony was grateful, because the parts of her legs that were visible were gnarled and knotted like two tree trunks. She wore a pair of very old carpet slippers three sizes too big for her. This whole sartorial get-up was crowned with a head of hair that could only have been a wig; it was half a shade off bright red and, from where he was sitting, looked to have the consistency of wire wool. He suddenly realised that she was speaking to him and dragged himself back to awareness.

"I'm sorry," he said. "What did you say?"

"I said all this must be very dull for you. Would you like to go and unpack?"

"Yes . . . thank you. Thank you very much."

"Pull the tiger's tail," said Mummy.

"I beg your pardon."

"The tiger's tail. It's a bell. Benskin will come and show you to your room." Feeling a complete idiot, Anthony did as he was told, jerking the tail of the tiger hard.

"I've put you in the blue room," said Mummy. "I hope you like blue."

"I love blue," said Anthony. He loathed blue.

"If you come back down in twenty minutes Dad'll be here."

"Fine," said Anthony. "Thank you very much."

A moment later the door opened and Benskin came in. "Madam?" he said.

"Show Mr. Bridges to his room, Benskin."

Benskin bowed and then stood aside as Anthony walked past him into the hall. He closed the drawing room doors behind him, and then headed across to the stairs, with Anthony following.

"Madam has put you in the blue room, sir," said Benskin.

"So she told me," said Anthony.

"I hope you like blue, sir."

"I love it."

"That's all right then," said Benskin, leading the way up the sweep of staircase to the first-floor landing.

"Been here long, Benskin?" asked Anthony, genuinely interested in how this personification of all that was best in butlers could possibly stand to work for someone like Mummy.

"Twenty-seven years, sir."

"Interesting job I should think," said Anthony.

"Extremely interesting, sir."

"Interesting lady, Mrs. Henshawe."

"Indeed so, sir."

"And Mr. Henshawe?"

"Sir?"

"Interesting?"

"Very interesting, sir."

"Mm," said Anthony, and that seemed to be that. He followed Benskin down what seemed like half a mile of corridor, until the butler threw open a pair of double doors and stepped back.

"The blue room, sir," he announced. Anthony walked in and was hard put to it not to recoil in horror. He was still standing there with his mouth open when he heard Benskin quietly close the doors behind him. The room was the bluest goddam blue he had ever seen. Everything was blue, the walls, the ceilings, the carpet, the furniture, the paintings; even the large mirror against one wall was tinted blue. And so that the overall effect wouldn't be spoiled by allowing some other colour to obtrude, the windows opening out on to the rear grounds were also tinted blue, so that the gardens beyond seemed to be studded with blue trees growing out of blue grass. In the distance Anthony could see a small blue gardener pruning some blue roses, while a little blue dog played around his feet. Without really having to look, Anthony checked the colour of the bed linen beneath the blue bedspread; blue sheets, blue pillow cases. A door set into one wall led through into the blue bathroom with its blue bathtub, blue toilet and blue bidet. The toilet paper was blue; so were the soap and the towels and the tissues and the toothpaste tube and the toothbrush. He walked back into the bedroom and stared around him, feeling a headache coming on. Then he lifted his hands up and looked at them; due to the filter provided by the tinted windows, his hands, too, looked blue and suddenly he decided that he couldn't stand it any longer. He stepped over to the door and opened it, walking out into the corridor once more. Sod the unpacking, he thought, I'll do it later. But he didn't want to go back downstairs just yet. .He would have to make excuses, and for the life of him he couldn't think what he would say. Instead, he would stay up here and prowl around a little. After all, he was a guest in this impossible mausoleum; nobody was going to accuse him of spying or trying to make off with the silver.

He headed back in the general direction of the staircase, but lost himself before he reached it. He must have made a left turn instead of a right somewhere back there. So he retraced his steps, made another left turn and realised that now he was truly lost; he couldn't even find his way back to his own bedroom. He listened outside a door for a couple of seconds and, hearing nothing, opened it. Jesus Christ, this was the pink room; a facsimile of his own room with the one basic difference. He closed the door quickly wondering how many other guest rooms had been decorated with the same lunatic taste. Then he heard voices. They were coming from a little way down the corridor he was standing in. Benskin probably; he'll put me right, thought Anthony. Perhaps if I slip him a fiver, he might change my bedroom without telling Mummy. Then he realised that he didn't have a fiver and, even if he had, he doubted that a mere fiver would be sufficient to tempt Benskin into disloyalty. But at least he'll point me towards the stairs, thought Anthony, so he headed in the direction of the voices. He made another left turn in the passage and ahead of him there was an open door. It was from there the voices were coming. Male and female, one of each.

"Jesus Christ!" said the male voice. "Can't you do anything right?"

Not Benskin, decided Anthony; the voice carried the trace of an American accent.

"If you told me what you wanted, I'd know what to do." Female voice this time, strangely garbled.

Then the male voice once more. "You're not supposed to blow. 'Blow' is just an expression."

Anthony tried to backtrack, but it was too late; he was already in the doorway. Perhaps if the man had been looking in some other direction, he might have been able to escape without being seen but, as it was, he found himself face to face with a stocky, totally bald, extremely naked man, with the bluest eyes he had ever seen, locked in a most peculiar embrace with a slim blonde girl. He raised a hand in a brief greeting to Anthony and then returned to his preoccupation.

Anthony fled. He ran down what seemed like a mile of corridor until he suddenly found himself at the top of the main stairs. He pulled himself together slowly, and was about to start downwards when the drawing room doors opened and Lilian and Mummy came out. Mummy spotted him immediately.

"Did you find Dad?" she called.

God, I hope not, prayed Anthony.

"No, Mrs. Henshawe."

"Never mind, he'll be down in a few minutes. Me and Lil are going for a walk in the garden. Why don't you go in the study and help yourself to a drink?"

"Thank you. I'd like that very much," said Anthony, in what he considered the understatement of the decade.

28

"Through the doors over there," said Mummy, and she and Lilian disappeared out of the front door.

*   *   *

Obviously Mummy's interior decorator hadn't been allowed to set foot in the study, because it was a magnificent room. Books lined one entire wall; there was a huge, elegant desk set in the centre of the room; deep leather armchairs; soft pools of light. One wall was given over to a single, large painting which looked as though it could be a Turner and which on closer inspection proved to be just that; there was also a Van Gogh, a small Rembrandt, two Renoirs and a blue period Picasso. All this, Anthony discovered after he had downed his first drink, which he had needed like he had never needed a drink before. The second drink went down almost as smoothly, and he was well into the third when the door opened and Daddy came in, cold blue eyes, bald head and all.

"Hi, young fella!" he said, heading for the bar.

Anthony scrambled to his feet. "How do you do, sir? I say . . . I'm terribly sorry about . . . terribly sorry."

Daddy waved the apologies away casually. "Think nothing of it. Happens all the time. Freshen your drink?"

"No sir, thank you."

Daddy poured himself a huge drink and carried it across to the desk. "Sit down, boy," he said. "You make me nervous hopping about like that."

Anthony realised that he was moving from one foot to the other like an embarrassed schoolboy up before the headmaster. He sat down in one of the armchairs and tried to look casual and at ease. "I've been admiring your pictures, sir," he said.

29

Daddy sat down and, tilting his chair back, put his feet on the desk. Anthony noticed with another twinge of horror that he wore no shoes or socks; but at least he had got his trousers on this time, which was a relief.

"Million and a half dollars' worth hanging right here," said Daddy.

"I'm not at all surprised," said Anthony, who knew a little about paintings.

"You've been banging my daughter," said Daddy, without a change of expression.

"I . . . we're very good friends," said Anthony.

"She's quite a lay," said Daddy. He *couldn't* have, thought Anthony; then he realised that nothing would surprise him any more. "Had a young fella in here once who told me she was the best goddam lay he'd ever had."

"We're very fond of each other, sir," said Anthony.

"Got to be to shack up with her for three months. Or is it the bread?"

"I beg your pardon?"

"Come on, boy, you're not all that stupid. What's the attraction? My little girl or my money?"

Fortified to some extent by the third drink, Anthony tried to muster some dignity. "It's certainly not the money, sir."

"Why not? You've got none of your own."

Hello, thought Anthony, someone has been nosing around. "I admit I'm not working at the moment, sir. But it's only temporary."

Daddy's icy blue eyes regarded him steadily across the desk. Anthony shifted his gaze to a point just above and between them; he found it less intimidating.

"And now you want to marry her?" said Daddy, suddenly.

30

"I do not," said Anthony, far too vehemently. He tried to soften it. "We haven't talked about it," he added.

"So what are you doing down here?"

"I really don't know. It was Lilian's idea."

"And you don't want to marry her?"

"Not particularly."

"Why not?"

Anthony shrugged. "I just don't want to get married right now."

"She does. She wants to marry you."

"Oh dear," said Anthony, who hadn't realised that things had gone that far.

"At least we agree on something," said Daddy. "You don't want to marry her, and I don't want her to marry you."

Anthony started to bristle slightly. "What's wrong with me?"

"You're a layabout. You haven't got a job and you've never had one worth ten cents. You're oversexed and under-talented."

Anthony thought about this for a moment; finally he was forced to agree.

"Yes sir, you're right," he said.

"I can see your point of view though," said Daddy. "You've got a good thing going for you at the moment. A permanent lay, and all found. It's going to take something pretty powerful to blast you away from all that."

My God, thought Anthony, he's going to bribe me to leave his daughter alone. The liquor he had consumed evaporated, and he started to concentrate. A deal was about to be made, and he wanted to be in full possession of all his faculties. He nodded his head. "Yes sir, something pretty powerful."

Daddy swung his chair round, putting his bare feet on the floor. He pulled open one of the desk drawers, took out a visiting card and flipped it towards Anthony. It was an expert trick; the card spun in the air and landed neatly in Anthony's lap. He looked at the card. There was nothing on it other than a telephone number, neatly engraved across the centre.

"Call that number next week. Speak to Walpole."

Anthony looked up from the card. "Speak about what, sir?"

"He'll know."

'I'd like to know, too, sir."

"Don't get stroppy with me, boy."

"I'm not getting stroppy, honestly."

Daddy looked at him shrewdly for a moment. "Lookit, boy," he said finally. "You don't want to marry my daughter. So that's fine by me. I go along with that. You've seen that revolting old cow I'm married to. I wouldn't wish marriage on my worst enemy. At the same time, you need something to shake you loose from that mink lined fornicator's paradise my little girl provides. Walpole will put you right."

"Yes sir, but who is Walpole, and what is he going to do?"

"He works for me. He'll give you a job."

Anthony must have looked a bit disappointed. "It's no good my offering you a few thousand dollars to pack your bags. My little girl would want to know where the money came from; you'd have to tell her, and then I'm up shit creek without a paddle. This way you tell her you've got a job; you've got to go abroad, and that's it. Besides, if you work at it, you can make a lot more than a few thousand dollars."

"What sort of job, sir?" asked Anthony, feeling that a few thousand dollars would have been infinitely preferable.

"Walpole will fix it," said Daddy. And before Anthony

could think of anything else to say, the door to the study opened and in walked the girl he had last seen upstairs with Daddy. "Hi, honey!" said Daddy. "Come and meet Anthony."

The girl came towards Anthony, who had got to his feet as she came in. She was an astonishingly beautiful little thing, with a neat, trim figure and pale blue eyes. She stuck out her hand.

"Hello, Anthony. My name's Shirleen."

"How do you do, Shirleen?" said Anthony.

Daddy, watching them with a smile, broke in, "Anything you'd like her to do for you, Anthony, my boy, just say the word. She's not much good yet, but she's learning fast."

For the second time that day, Anthony fled. Not so much because of what Daddy was offering as because he suddenly found Shirleen irresistibly attractive and was afraid he might accept.

*   *   *

The remainder of the weekend passed with agonising slowness. Anthony knew that if he lived to be a hundred and four, he would never forget it. Every single detail was imprinted indelibly on his memory. There were the highlights of course, like the fact that Mummy and Daddy never spoke a single word to one another direct, conducting their conversation solely through the imperturbable Benskin; and the moment on Sunday morning when Mummy walked into the Blue Room without knocking, catching him and Lilian in what Lilian liked to call her "setting up exercises". Mummy had simply told them not to be late for Church, and walked out again.

*   *   *

They were silent for most of the return drive to London. They reached the outskirts of Putney before Lilian said anything.

"Enjoy yourself?"

"Fascinating," said Anthony.

"They're a little eccentric, I know, but they're dears," said Lilian. And that was the one and only reference she ever made to the weekend.

2 :::

ANTHONY HAD LEFT IT UNTIL TUESDAY TO CALL
the number Daddy had given him. Then, after Lilian had
gone to have her hair done, he had dialled the number. The
phone had rung once the other end before being picked up.

"Yes?" A female voice.

"Mr. Walpole, please."

"Who's calling?"

"Mr. Bridges. Anthony Bridges."

"Wait." The line went dead for a few seconds, and then
a male voice came on. "Yes?"

"Mr. Walpole?"

"Yes."

"Mr. Bridges here."

"Lunch. Twelve-thirty," and the phone was replaced the other end.

Anthony re-dialled. "Mr. Bridges here again," he said. "I'm lunching with Mr. Walpole but he didn't say where."

"Here," said the female voice. "Mr. Walpole always lunches here."

"But where is here?" said Anthony, starting to feel desperate. "One-three-five, Pandam Street. Don't be late." And the phone was hung up once more.

Anthony brushed off his one and only dark blue suit, sewed a button on the most respectable shirt he owned and polished up his shoes. Then he counted his loose change to see whether he could afford a taxi. He decided that he couldn't, and as Lilian never kept any money around the house, it would have been useless looking. He found Pandam Street in the London street map, borrowed from the man next door, and worked out that he could get there by Tube if he changed at Charing Cross, and if he didn't mind a short walk. He allowed himself thirty-five minutes for the journey, and at twelve-thirty exactly he was standing outside 135 Pandam Street.

*　　　　*　　　　*

It was one of those tiny streets that festoon the City of London. No. 135 was crouched between a seedy looking coffee bar and an equally seedy looking office equipment shop. The building itself was three storeys high and looked sadly in need of demolition. There was a grimy brass plate screwed to the edge of the door lintel with the name H. WALPOLE engraved on to it. There was nothing else; nothing to say who or what Mr. Walpole did for a living. Anthony pulled his cuffs down, rubbed his shoes briefly on the backs

36

of his trouser legs, and pushed open the outer door. He found himself in a dusty looking corridor with some stairs at the far end and a couple of doors leading from it. One of them had a card pinned on it. KNOCK AND ENTER. So he knocked and entered. The room he found himself in was large and, apart from the overcrowding provided by the furnishings, empty. He stood there for a moment, not quite sure what to do next.

"Anyone home?" he risked finally. There was no answer.

He walked back into the passage once more. "Hello there," he called, louder this time. "Anyone around?"

"Stop shouting, you'll disturb Mr. Walpole."

He turned quickly as a woman came in from the street. She was about forty-five years old, stocky, with hair cut short, too much make-up and thick-rimmed glasses. She was wearing a tweedy sort of suit which didn't fit her too well, and carrying a paper bag in one hand with the words "Cohen's Delicatessen" printed on it. "I'm sorry," said Anthony. "I couldn't find anyone."

"I was out," she said, walking through into the office Anthony had just come from.

Anthony followed her in. 'My name is Bridges. I have an appointment with Mr. Walpole.'

"I know, I know," she said testily. "You'll have to wait."

Anthony watched as she busied herself with the paper bag. She took out two paper plates and a couple of packages wrapped in greaseproof paper which she unwrapped to disclose half a dozen substantial looking sandwiches; these she divided equally between the two plates. Suddenly she looked up from her work, straight at Anthony. "I hope you like salt beef," she said.

Anthony admitted that he quite liked it.

"It's kosher," she said.

"I'm not Jewish," said Anthony, not quite sure why he bothered.

"Neither is Mr. Walpole. He has salt beef sandwiches every day," she said.

Anthony had been looking forward to an expense account lunch, at the Caprice or Mirabelle at least, and his stomach growled a small protest at the thought of salt beef sandwiches. He watched while the woman laid small paper napkins on the plates. Then she reached into a filing cabinet and pulled out a bottle.

"Dill pickle?" she snapped at Anthony.

"Please," he answered.

She laid one pickle on each plate, then stood back to admire the effect. Apparently satisfied, she picked up the plates and headed for the door again.

"Follow me," she said as she walked out.

Anthony followed her into the passage and up the stairs. At the top was a small landing with two doors leading from it; a further flight of stairs led up to the second floor. The woman approached one of the doors and, turning her back to it, she knocked on it with the heel of her shoe.

"Enter," came a voice from inside. The woman started to juggle with the two plates, trying to free one hand long enough to open the door.

Anthony hurried forward. "Here, let me."

"I can manage, thank you," she said with awful venom.

Anthony stepped back and waited for his lunch to slide from the plate on to the floor, but she managed the operation without losing anything. She disappeared into the office and kicked the door shut behind her. Anthony stood looking around at the dingy, institutional brown walls, the scuffed linoleum and the peeling paintwork. He tried to reconcile his surroundings with a business empire that enabled its founder to hang a million and a half dollars' worth of paintings in one room. He couldn't do it. A muted sound of voices came from behind the door and somewhere in the building Anthony could hear a telephone ringing. Then he turned as the door at the end of the corridor opened suddenly and someone peered out. It was a little old man, straight out of Dickens, with a wing collar, black jacket, celluloid cuffs and pince-nez. He blinked towards Anthony for a couple of seconds.

"I thought I heard someone," he said. Then he disappeared again, slamming the door behind him. And at that moment the woman came out again.

"You can go in now," she said. "Do you like sugar in your tea?"

"No thank you," said Anthony. "Just milk."

"Mm," she said, as though Anthony had asked for something dirty. Then she stood aside and Anthony walked into the office.

It was a large room with more junk in it than Anthony had ever seen in one place. Books, ledgers, papers and files were piled everywhere; against the walls, on the chairs, under the windows, on and under small tables, and on one large table set across the far corner of the room. Of Mr. Walpole there was no sign. Anthony turned to the woman for guidance, but she had already closed the door behind him. He faced into the room once more and cleared his throat, hoping the sound would flush out Mr. Walpole.

"Don't just stand there. Come and sit down," came the voice.

Looking towards the large table in the corner, Anthony saw what looked like the top of a bald head just visible over a pile of ledgers. As though to confirm his sighting, the head moved and Anthony saw a face peering at him from behind the screen of books.

"Sit there," said Walpole.

By "there" Anthony assumed he meant a small cane-bottomed chair in front of the table which was miraculously empty of books and papers. "Good morning, sir," he said. moving towards the chair, trying at the same time to see what Mr. Walpole looked like.

"It's past noon," said Mr. Walpole. "Good afternoon."

"Yes, sir," said Anthony, sitting down. "Good afternoon."

At last he could see Walpole. Anthony had an instant classification method he used when he met people for the first time; it involved comparing them to animals. There were the pussy cat people; the doggy people; the bird people; and the crocodile people. There were all sorts of subdivisions of the classifications, but they usually came later when he knew the people better. Walpole fitted so perfectly into his classification that Anthony didn't think he would ever need to revise or subdivide it; he was crocodile, plain and simple. He even looked like a crocodile. There was no way of estimating how tall he was from behind the table, but he was very, very thin. His face was strangely elongated and narrow as though it had been squeezed in a vice, forcing the features forward. His eyes were mud coloured, his nose enormous, his teeth uneven and not particularly clean, his mouth practically non-existent, his ears tiny and pressed very close to his head; his complexion was grey and the few strands of hair on either side of his head were grey, too. His neck was wrinkled and the backs of his hands were scaly; his fingernails were very long and beautifully manicured. He was wearing a black jacket, white shirt with stiff collar and a grey silk necktie.

Now that Anthony could see him clearly, he decided that Mr. Walpole was easily the most unattractive person he had ever met, Mummy notwithstanding. Walpole gazed at him for a long moment, then he abruptly pushed one of the paper plates towards him.

"Your lunch," he said.

"Thank you, sir," said Anthony, having lost his appetite. Walpole didn't seem to have done so however, because he picked up a sandwich and took an enormous bite from it. Then, with his mouth full and crumbs spilling down the front of his jacket, he said something.

"I beg your pardon, sir?" said Anthony who hadn't been able to understand a word through its salt beef sandwich filter.

Walpole chewed for a moment; then swallowed. "I said, 'So you want to come and work for us do you?'"

"That seems to be the idea, sir," said Anthony brightly.

"Well do you, or don't you?"

"Yes, sir. Please," said Anthony.

"What can you do?"

Anthony spread his hands in a deprecating gesture. "Practically anything."

"Can you design or build a dam?"

"No, sir, I don't think so."

"Can you sink an oil well?"

"Not really."

"Can you fly a jet?"

"As a matter of fact sir, no."

"Can you run a rubber plantation?"

"Actually I've never tried."

"Can you prospect for gold, boss a lumber camp, tell the difference between high and low grade uranium ore, design

41

an oil refinery, run an off-shore rig, speak fluent Spanish, Hebrew, Russian, Chinese or Hindustani?"

"Unfortunately not," said Anthony.

Walpole took another giant bite from his sandwich and chewed it for a couple of moments before swallowing it. "When you say you can do practically anything, what you really mean is practically nothing," he said, finally.

"Those were pretty specialised things you were asking me about, sir," said Anthony, realising that he was going to have a bit of a struggle on his hands.

"We run a specialised business here, young man," said Walpole. "Eat your sandwiches!"

Not wanting to appear completely discourteous, Anthony started to nibble at a sandwich while Walpole devoured the remainder of his.

"Why do you want to work for us?" he asked finally.

At that moment Anthony couldn't think of anything he wanted to do less, but he persevered. "It was Mr. Henshawe's idea actually," he said.

"I know it was. He told me. I suppose you've been sniffing around his daughter?"

Steady on, thought Anthony. "I am acquainted with Miss Henshawe, yes," he said, with as much dignity as he could muster at such short notice.

"Mm," said Walpole. "You're not the first."

There was another long silence, during which the woman from downstairs crashed into the office with two cups of luke-warm tea. After she had left, Walpole seemed to come to some sort of a decision.

"Mr. Henshawe wants you employed. So employed you will be. At what, I have no idea at present. On your way out collect a form from the office next door. Fill it out and post it to me. You'll be hearing from me."

Anthony realised that the interview was over. He left the office as quickly as he could, glad to have been spared the remainder of the salt beef sandwiches. Outside he walked along the passage and tapped on the door at the end.

"Please come in," said a voice.

Anthony opened the door and walked in. The office was smaller than Walpole's, but otherwise identical, complete to the books and papers strewn everywhere. The little man Anthony had seen earlier was sorting through a stack of ledgers. He looked up as Anthony came in. Definitely bird people, thought Anthony; like a little sparrow.

"Yes? Yes?" said the little man.

"Mr. Walpole said I was to collect a form from you."

The man nodded towards a corner of the office. "Over there," he said.

Anthony walked in the indicated direction towards a huge pile of printed papers in six different colours. He stood in front of the papers for a moment then turned back to the little man who seemed to have forgotten his existence.

"Excuse me. What sort of form do I need?"

The little man looked up. "Don't you know?" Anthony shook his head. The man clicked his tongue a couple of times and shook his head. "Well what are you doing, young man?" he asked. "Are you going out to Calcutta? Are you flying in to Biafra? Do you need traveller's cheques, sovereigns, gold bars, dollars, small-pox injections, a new passport, a gun permit, diplomatic immunity? What is it you want?"

"A job," said Anthony.

"White forms on the bottom, headed Employment Questionnaire," said the little man, returning to his business.

Anthony extracted one of the forms; then, just to be on the safe side, he took another one.

"Thank you," he said as he walked to the door.

"Don't slam the door," said the little man without looking up.

As Anthony came out into the passage, the woman from downstairs was coming from Walpole's office carrying the remains of Anthony's salt beef sandwiches. She glared at Anthony. "I hate waste," she said, and stomped down the stairs ahead of him. Anthony took one further look around the place and then escaped into the afternoon sunshine.

* * *

"But what *sort* of things does he do?" said Anthony for the tenth time.

"Why are you so interested all of a sudden?" said Lilian.

They were sitting in bed together. Lilian was doing her nails. She always liked to do something constructive after sex, whereas Anthony only ever wanted to sleep. Anthony shrugged in a show of indifference.

"I'm not really interested; just curious." In fact he was desperately interested. From what he had seen of Daddy's enterprises he wasn't at all sure that he wanted to become part of them; certainly not until he found out a lot more about what went on.

"I've told you. He buys and sells things," said Lilian.

"And?"

"He builds things."

"Like dams?"

"Do you like this shade?" She held up her hand for inspection, but Anthony wasn't to be sidetracked.

"And gold mines and oil wells?"

44

"You don't build oil wells or gold mines. You sink them," said Lilian, starting on the other hand.

"All right. Does he sink them?"

"I suppose so. I could ask Mummy."

"Why Mummy?"

"Daddy never does anything without telling Mummy."

That's what you think, thought Anthony. "In that case I may as well ask Benskin," he said. "He's their interpreter."

"You could, but he wouldn't tell you anything," said Lilian. "He's on to a good thing there. He's not going to let anyone else join."

"You mean he knows *all* your father's business?"

"If it's been discussed with Mummy he does. And its usually been discussed. She's very bright." She blew on her fingernails. "Nearly dry," she said. "Hey, I read something in *Kama Sutra* yesterday. It's called Lotus Blossom Climbing. Let's give it a try."

Why not? thought Anthony. Perhaps it would be best to forget the whole business and leave things as they are. Lilian hadn't mentioned anything more about marriage since the "weekend"; perhaps she would be willing to let things slide on the way they were. In which case there was no need to worry about going to work for Daddy or anyone else. They tried Lotus Blossom Climbing, and it turned out to be rather dull.

*   *   *

Anthony paused for a moment before dropping the questionnaire in the letter box. He had put it off until the last possible moment, but in the last couple of days Lilian had been coming on too strong for him to ignore it any longer. It

45

had started three days ago, just after he had definitely decided that he wasn't going to work for Daddy. She had got the curse, and she was usually grotty for a couple of days during her period; but this time she excelled herself.

"I want to get married," she said suddenly – and then continued to say it at every opportunity. Anthony had tried to talk her out of it, gently at first, moving on to the stage of flat refusal, and finally finishing by yelling at her that he wouldn't marry her if she were the last woman on earth. This wasn't true, because he really was quite fond of her, but he couldn't stand the thought of being married to anyone except the beautiful lady of his dreams. So they had shouted and yelled at each other, and finally Anthony had dug through the wastepaper basket and found the discarded questionnaire. He had filled it in secretly, hoping all the time that something would occur to obviate the necessity of his posting it. But nothing had. If things went on the way they were, he was going to have to do one of two things; marry Lilian, or move out. And with no money, job or prospects, he had nowhere to move out to. All he had was the vague unknown that was wrapped up in the questionnaire. He looked at the envelope once more, raised his eyes to heaven in a silent prayer, and stuck it in the letter box before he had time to change his mind again.

3

"WHY DIDN'T YOU TELL ME YOU HAD BEEN IN THE
army?" said Walpole.

"You didn't give me a chance to tell you anything, sir."
replied Anthony.

Walpole looked at him from his mud coloured eyes, then
back down at the questionnaire he was holding. "There's
nothing else here of the slightest interest. I can't understand
why you didn't tell me?"

He's making a mountain out of a molehill, thought
Anthony. "I was only in for three years," he said.

"You say here you were an officer."

"Second Lieutenant."

"Why didn't you stay in?"

Actually Anthony would have liked to have remained in the army; he had enjoyed the life, completely free of all responsibility or necessity to think for himself; but he had been requested politely but firmly to leave when his term was up.

"The military life was too restricting," he said to Walpole.

"What did you learn about guns?" asked Walpole.

"Guns?"

"Guns. You were a soldier. You must have seen a gun."

"Yes, sir. I learned how to fire them."

"What sort?"

"Rifle. Revolver. Anti-tank gun, zabooka."

"Bazooka."

"Yes, sir; bazooka."

"Were you any good?"

"Sir?"

"Did you ever hit anything?"

He had been terrible. The Sergeant Instructor had invariably ordered the entire range cleared of personnel whenever he saw Anthony approach. "I was pretty good, sir. Actually, very good."

"Have you got a passport?"

"Yes, sir."

"Bring it in next time you come. Now go next door and see Millwright. Tell him you're working for Hengun Incorporated."

"Er . . . shouldn't we talk about terms . . . salary, things like that?" asked Anthony, hopefully.

"Standard contract. Five thousand pounds a year paid into an account in Switzerland, all expenses and a one per cent commission on direct sales," said Walpole, pushing the questionnaire aside and taking up different papers. "Good day, Mr. Bridges."

Without quite knowing how, Anthony found himself out in the passage. He wanted a drink badly; more, he *needed* a drink. He felt like going back in and asking Walpole to repeat what he had just said. Five thousand a year! Surely he must have meant dollars? But he had said pounds, and he certainly wasn't the kind of man to make that sort of mistake. Paid in Switzerland; even Anthony knew that meant tax free; all expenses, whatever it meant, couldn't be bad; one per cent commission didn't sound too generous, but there was no point worrying about it until he knew what he would be earning his commission against. My God! Five thousand a year tax free! He was a bloody millionaire and he still had no idea what he was going to have to do to earn it. He tapped on the far door.

"Please come in."

He went in. "Mr. Millwright?"

The little man seemed to be searching for the same thing he had been ten days ago. "Yes, what is it?"

"Mr. Walpole asked me to tell you that I am working for Hengun Incorporated."

"Hengun, Hengold, Henstruction, Henoil. Why don't we just call the whole thing Henshawe? It would save me a great deal of time and trouble." He had moved over to another pile of papers while he was talking; now he looked up at Anthony across the top of his pince-nez. "Hengun, you said?"

"Yes, sir."

"Here you are then." He pulled a couple of sheets of paper from the bottom of the pile, glanced at them briefly, then handed them to Anthony. "Sit over there; read it; then sign it. Right?"

"Yes, sir," said Anthony.

He took the papers over to the window, cleared a few books off a chair, sat down and started to read. It was a printed form, pages one and two of a contract. The main heading read HENGUN INCORPORATED followed by a P.O. box address in Dallas, Texas. Then there was a sub-heading: Terms of Employment. Beneath that, the small print started. There were fifteen numbered paragraphs and Anthony read them through quickly; then he started at the top and read them through again. After that he stared out of the window for a couple of minutes; then he read them once more. Finally he cleared his throat. Millwright had found what he was looking for and was now perched at a high old fashioned desk, copying items into a ledger. He jumped at the sound Anthony made.

"I'd forgotten you were there," he said irritably. "You've made me smudge an entry."

"Sorry," said Anthony. "There's a couple of things I don't quite understand."

"It's all perfectly clear."

"I know. But I'd still like them explained. Like here, in paragraph twelve. 'The party of the second part' – that's me. 'If the party of the second part is arrested, apprehended, taken prisoner, brought into custody; and if as a result of the aforementioned he is subsequently brought before a Court of Law, military or civilian, howsoever convened; then the party of the first part' – that's Hengun – 'will disclaim, and/or disavow any knowledge of the party of the second part' – that's me." He looked up towards Millwright hopefully.

"It seems perfectly clear to me," snapped Millwright. "If you're caught, Hengun denies that you exist."

"I understand that," said Anthony. "But what will I be doing? Is it illegal?"

50

Millwright's mouth cracked open in an imitation of a smile. "That depends where you're doing it, doesn't it?" he said.

Anthony realised that he wasn't going to get very far with Millwright, but he persevered. "Paragraph eight. 'The party of the second part' – me – 'will take full responsibility for any or all of the consignments in his charge, and will be held financially responsible for their loss or damage howsoever caused. However, the party of the first part will, in special circumstances, waive their rights on any amount over the value of one million dollars.' "

"Perfectly clear," said Millwright. "Hengun will accept anything over the first million dollars' loss. You will be expected to make up any amount under that."

"I thought that's what it said," agreed Anthony. "But what does it *mean*?"

Millwright smiled again; the old bastard is really enjoying himself, thought Anthony. "It means that you had better be very careful, young man, that's what it means."

"Paragraph six. 'In the event of the death of the party of the second part, his personal accounts will be sealed forthwith. After payment of all monies due to Hengun, the balance, less ten per cent handling charges, will be paid to the named next of kin.' "

"Ten per cent is quite reasonable," said Millwright.

"I'm sure it is," said Anthony. "It's not that I'm worrying about. I just wondered why it is considered necessary to mention death at all. I mean, it's not dangerous is it?"

"What?"

"The job."

"That will depend what you make of it, won't it?"

Beginning to feel a little desperate, Anthony turned back

51

to the contract. "Paragraph fifteen. 'Any dispute under this contract shall be settled according to the laws of Lamboola.' What's Lamboola?"

"It's a small country on the West Coast of Africa."

"I've never heard of it."

"Not many people have," said Millwright, almost chuckling out loud.

"What's wrong with the laws of England or America?"

"Oh dear me," said Millwright. "They're not nearly so beneficial."

"Beneficial to who . . . whom?"

About here, Millwright decided that he had said enough. "I can't sit here all day talking to you young man," he said. "Now sign the contract. I'll witness it and Mr. Walpole will sign it on behalf of Hengun."

"I'm not sure that I want to sign it," said Anthony.

Millwright seemed to lose interest. "Very well. Leave it there and don't slam the door on the way out."

"Perhaps I ought to speak to Mr. Henshawe about it."

"Oh I doubt it," said Millwright. "I doubt it very much."

You're probably right, thought Anthony. He glanced at the contract once more and weighed up the pros and cons. He had burned his bridges as far as Lilian was concerned; even if he did a complete about-face and offered to marry her, it was doubtful now whether she would accept him. The last few days they had been crucifying each other with words, nailing them in hard and fast. He had walked out twice and she had thrown him out once. I don't just burn bridges, he thought, I demolish them. And after all, his prospective employers had a right to protect themselves; they didn't know Anthony from a hole in the ground. Walpole had called it a standard contract which meant that everyone who worked for Hengun signed the same thing. And there was that five thousand a year tax free.

Anthony pulled out his pen and signed.

* * *

The next few days passed in a blur. He delivered his passport to Millwright, who checked it carefully and then gave him forms to fill in applying for visas for fifteen different countries, three of which Anthony had never even heard of. He spent a day hanging round a Harley Street surgery getting inoculated against every disease known to medical science; then he spent two days in bed getting over the inoculations. He was presented with two hundred and fifty pounds expense money and told to check in to the Manchip Hotel in the Bayswater Road, where a room had been reserved and paid for. He went from Embassy to Embassy, watching his passport being stamped on page after page. It seemed that the smaller the country, the larger and more ornate the visa required to visit it. When any of the Consular officials asked the purpose of his intended visit to their country, he would hand over a letter Millwright had given him. The letter was almost invariably addressed to the First Secretary, and in two cases to the Ambassador himself. It always did the trick; no more questions were asked; his passport was stamped with the appropriate visa and he was practically bowed out of the place. He collected credit cards; Diners, American Express, Carte Blanche, Bankamerica, two airline credit cards, a Hertz card, an Avis card, two gasoline company cards and a card he had never seen before entitling him to cash a personal cheque up to one thousand dollars in any branch of any bank, anywhere in the world. And finally, he shook himself loose from Lilian.

"I'm moving out," he said.

"Again?"

"I've got a job."

"Ha!"

He was packing his things, and still she didn't believe him. But he didn't want to leave a sour taste, so he tried to explain to her how reasonable he was being.

"We've had a marvellous time these last few months. Let's try to part without too many recriminations." She had dissolved into tears.

"But I love you! I love you! I love you!"

"No, you don't," said Anthony, not really believing it. "You're fond of me, as I am of you. But you don't love me."

"Yes I do."

"You just think you do."

Then she had made things easier by hitting him with the box of tissues she had been rifling. If nothing else, his dignity had been hurt and he finished his packing quickly and walked out without a backward glance. His ego was slightly dented by hearing her on the 'phone just as he left.

"Yes, I'd love to. Anthony? I haven't seen Anthony for days. We're through, didn't you know? He was so insecure it was sickening. Fine, pick me up at seven."

But, in spite of this, it was a relief. He wasn't quite sure yet where he was going with Hengun Inc., but at least it was in a completely new direction. He whistled tunelessly to himself as he hailed a taxi. The sun was shining, the weather balmy; he had two hundred and fifty pounds in his pocket, a Swiss bank account, and not a soul in the world to concern himself with; he couldn't wait to get started at his new job, and if

54

someone would only tell him what it was, he would be completely happy.

Two weeks later, he was still waiting.

*   *   *

God, how he hated his hotel room. He hated the entire hotel for that matter; the cool, efficient, impersonal service; the very good food; the sheer bloody comfort of the place. He had been delighted with the whole set-up when he arrived, but he had been told to hold himself ready at the end of the telephone twenty-four hours a day and, being reasonably conscientious, he had done just that. For the first few days he had even enjoyed himself. He hated to admit it, but it was a relief to have got Lilian off his back; he was well and truly clapped out, and the enforced rest would do him good. Added to that had been the enjoyment of buying himself a new wardrobe. He couldn't see what else he was going to spend his two hundred and fifty pounds on, so he decided he would blow most of it on clothes. If anyone screamed at him later for misusing his expense money, he would tell them to stop it from his salary. He left a message at the hotel switchboard that he would be out for an hour or so and took a cab to the King's Road. There he went mad, spending close to two hundred pounds in just over half an hour. He raced back to the hotel, to be told that there had been no calls, and spent the next couple of hours trying on his new gear. Then his spirits dropped somewhat as he realised that he wouldn't be able to show it off. He called a couple of birds he used to know, but he had been out of circulation so long that one of them had forgotten who he was, and the other was getting married the following day; perhaps if he called next week? He even risked a call to Walpole after a few days.

55

"I'd like to go away for the weekend," he said.

"You can't." And that had been that.

Towards the middle of the second week he had started to feel the need for female companionship, so he took to hanging around the hotel bar, making sure the switchboard operator knew where he was. But the Manchip Hotel was one of those eminently respectable places whose female clientele all seemed to be over the age of forty-five and married to boot. There had been one brief fling with an American school teacher who had missed her connecting flight back to the States and been put up overnight in the Manchip by the airline. She had been very sweet and extremely grateful, but wholly unsatisfying, merely serving to whet the appetite. He had made a tentative pass at the attractive looking receptionist who covered the day shift; she turned out to be a tight assed little lesbian and, having drunk her way through half a bottle of his scotch, asked him if he had a girl friend handy, because she was feeling that way. For one wild, desperate evening he had considered calling Lilian, but reason prevailed and he had started to watch the television instead, going to bed at eleven each night, and trying to convince himself that he wasn't feeling what he knew bloody well he was feeling.

*　　　*　　　*

Exactly fifteen days after moving into the hotel he received his first telephone call. It was the woman who worked for Walpole whose name, he had learned, was Ada Cremin. He was in the shower when the phone rang, and at first he didn't hear it; then, as he turned off the water, he heard the ringing from his room. He leaped from the shower and, soaking wet, ran into the bedroom, sprawled across the bed and grabbed up the receiver.

"What took you so long to answer?" asked Miss Cremin.

"I was in the shower."

"It's past eleven o'clock." The tone of her voice said that only degenerates showered so late in the day.

"I am aware of the time, thank you," said Anthony, who felt that as an executive with the organisation they both worked for he wasn't getting sufficient respect from a mere secretary.

"Mr. Walpole wants to see you."

"When?"

"Lunch. Twelve-thirty." And she hung up. With visions of salt-beef sandwiches and luke-warm tea, Anthony got dressed slowly. He telephone downstairs for a cab, and forty-five minutes later he was on his way to Pandam Street.

*   *   *

Miss Cremin was busy arranging the sandwiches on their paper plates when Anthony came into her office.

"I hate waste," she said without preamble. "I've only bought you one sandwich."

"Thank you," said Anthony. "May I go up?"

"You most certainly can not." Anthony waited while she doled out the pickles; then followed her upstairs. She disappeared into Walpole's office and right on cue Millwright stuck his head out of the door at the end of the corridor. "I thought I heard somebody," he said, and slammed the door again. A moment later Miss Cremin came out and told Anthony that he could go in. Walpole peered around the pile of ledgers on his desk.

"Sit down," he said. Anthony sat. Walpole took at least

half his sandwich at a single bite and started to talk. Anthony was shaking his head before Walpole finished his first sentence. He gulped down the huge mouthful and asked, "You mean you won't?"

"Won't what?"

"What were you shaking your head for?"

"I'm sorry, sir. I couldn't understand what you were saying."

Walpole looked at him steadily for a moment as though Anthony were a complete cretin. Then he started again. "A *Señor* Ramirez is arriving at London Airport tonight. You will take care of him. Clear?"

"Not quite," said Anthony.

Walpole sighed almost imperceptibly. "You will meet him off the plane. You will escort him to his apartment. You will stay with him until he is ready to leave. Then you will escort him back to the airport. Now is it clear?"

"Yes, sir. I think so."

"Good." He pushed an envelope towards Anthony. "Here are his flight particulars, the keys to the apartment and five hundred pounds in cash which you will hand to him on arrival. You are to see that he has everything he wants, as and when he wants it."

"How long will Mr. Ramirez be staying in London?" Anthony enquired, not unreasonably.

"Until he leaves," said Walpole. "Good day."

Anthony was outside the office before he realised that he hadn't touched his salt beef sandwich. That would please Miss Cremin he thought, as he caught a taxi to the Caprice. There he lunched alone and at great expense.

*   *   *

58

Anthony was at the airport half an hour before the scheduled time of arrival of Ramirez's flight. He contacted a BOAC official and told him that he was meeting a Señor Ramirez; would the official please check the passengers and then identify Ramirez to him as they came through from customs. He told the chauffeur of the hired Rolls to watch the flight arrivals indicator and to have the car waiting outside the terminal fifteen minutes after the aircraft landed. Then he went to get himself a drink. He wouldn't admit it to himself, but he was choked. A bloody tourist guide, that's all he was Anthony Bridges, with his five thousand a year and his Swiss bank account, wet nursing some South American around London. Still, at least he was out of the hotel, which made a change. He ordered another drink, just as it was announced over the public address that Ramirez's flight would be one hour late due to technical difficulties. By the time the flight landed Anthony had consumed three more drinks and was feeling at peace with the world.

Ten minutes after the landing had been confirmed he walked downstairs and joined the people waiting for the disembarking passengers to come through from immigration and customs. He recognised his BOAC official as he came through the doors and looked at the man who accompanied him. Ramirez was tiny, a shade over five feet tall, and very slim. He was about forty years old, with a head of well oiled thick black hair, a small, neatly trimmed moustache, and dark brown eyes. He seemed as excited as a schoolboy on the first day of the vacation. The BOAC man turned him over to Anthony, who introduced himself.

Ramirez clicked his heels and bowed. "Carlos Santos Miguel Anthonio Ramirez."

"Where is your luggage, *Señor* Ramirez?" Anthony asked.

59

Ramirez held up a briefcase he was carrying. "Is all here."

"All?" said Anthony. The man had just flown three thousand odd miles; there *had* to be more.

"Is all," said Ramirez flashing his immaculate, gold studded teeth. "I am travelling lightly when I am coming to London because I am buying many clothes from your Saville Road and Marks and Spencers."

And putting them all down to expenses, thought Anthony. "Do you come to London often?" he asked, as they walked out to the car.

"I am not being here for three years now," said Ramirez. "I am being in prison, which makes it difficult to travel."

The chauffeur opened the door for them and they both got into the back of the Rolls. Anthony had already told the driver the address of the apartment, and he settled back for the thirty-five minute drive, content to be relaxing in the back of a Rolls with half a dozen drinks warming his insides. Ramirez was mostly quiet during the drive, but there was obviously a suppressed excitement bubbling around inside of him.

Thinking that he ought to make some conversation, Anthony pointed out some buildings that had gone up during the past three years. Ramirez was polite, but uninterested. Perhaps he would prefer to talk about himself, thought Anthony.

"How long have you been dealing with us. *Señor* Ramirez?" he asked

"Five. No, six years," said Carlos.

"That's a long time."

"And it will be longer, I am hoping. Our trade is one that goes on forever."

60

"I agree," said Anthony, hoping that a clue would emerge eventually. "It's a good trade."

"The best. It has been very good to me – if you are not including the prison."

"You didn't actually explain why you went to prison."

Carlos shrugged. "These things happen." he said. "The sides change quickly. They are changing too quickly for me this time. I am dealing with the power one day; the next day the power is no longer the power and I am in prison."

"Bad luck."

"Not so bad. They are wanting to shoot me at first. But I am pointing out that perhaps one day they would be having a use for me. They are thinking about this for a couple of days; and then they decide that I am right. So they don't shoot me. They are putting me in prison instead."

"Awkward," said Anthony.

Ramirez shrugged expressively. "Is an occupational blizzard," he said.

"Hazard?"

"*Si*. Hazard."

"Of course," said Anthony, as though he understood fully. But Ramirez had said "our" line of business! Did that include Anthony? Paragraph twelve of the contract swam before his eyes: "If the party of the second part is arrested, apprehended, taken prisoner . . .". He really would have to make a concrete effort tomorrow to find out what kind of business he was in, while he was still on the outside. Perhaps Ramirez could tell him. But on second thoughts it didn't seem a very good idea to ask. After all, he was supposed to be representing Hengun Inc., and it wouldn't be too bright to admit that he didn't have any idea of what he was supposed to be

61

doing. He resolved to try to find out subtly. If Ramirez was going to be around for a few days, it shouldn't be too difficult.

*　　　*　　　*

The apartment was in Shepherd's Market, just off Park Lane and in the shadow of the Hilton and the Playboy Club. Anthony had been given the keys and the address, but had not yet seen the place. The Rolls drew up outside the building and the chauffeur opened the door for them.

"Will you be requiring me further, sir?" he asked as Anthony got out. Why not? thought Anthony. He was obviously not expected to sit beside his telephone tonight, so he could do the town as soon as he had Ramirez bedded down. He told the driver to wait, and he and Ramirez walked up the two wide steps to the front door. It was open and it led into a small lobby reeking with opulence.

Flat three was on the second floor; in fact it *was* the second floor. At first count Anthony made it five bedrooms; the second count turned up a sixth behind the kitchen. Apart from the bedrooms and kitchen, there was an enormous living room, a study, and four bathrooms. The whole place was done out in a style which Anthony immediately classified as early Bordello. There was a preponderance of velvet and satin, and the basic colour was rich ruby red. There were mirrors everywhere, in ornate heavy gold frames; shaggy rugs were scattered all over the fitted carpets, and cushions littered the apartment from end to end. The bedrooms were like something from the erotic dreams of a Victorian profligate, with naked cherubs climbing up the bed posts, more mirrors, concealed lights, heavy brocade drapes, and opulent nudes hanging on the walls. Anthony toured the place slowly, savouring each new marvel as it presented itself. Not so

62

Ramirez though. He went through the entire apartment very quickly; then came back to find Anthony who had only just recovered from the second bedroom. His little face was downcast and he seemed ready to burst into tears.

"Where are the ladies?" he asked.

"I beg your pardon?"

"The ladies. They are not here."

"Which ladies do you mean, Mr. Ramirez?"

"The ladies. *Les poules. Las puntas.*"

"The whores?"

Ramirez smiled. "*Si, si.* The whores. Where are they?"

Anthony laughed; obviously Ramirez had a sense of humour. "I see what you mean," he said. "It *is* a bit like a Victorian brothel. Yes, very funny."

"They are coming soon?" said Ramirez, his eyes shining.

Anthony stopped laughing. "You mean it."

"Mean what?"

"What you said about the whores?"

"Of course I am meaning it. What you think I am. A fairy?" It was amazing how mean he could look for such a little man, thought Anthony. And what had Walpole said? "Everything he wants, when he wants it."

"I assumed that you would prefer to select your own company," said Anthony.

Ramirez digested this for a moment before dazzling Anthony with another show of teeth. "*Si.* I select. We go now." He took Anthony's arm and started to lead him towards the living room and front door.

But Anthony needed time. "Don't you want to freshen up after your flight?" he asked.

Ramirez gave this some thought, then he nodded. "*Si.* I freshen up so I do not stink when I meet the whores."

In what seemed to Anthony like fifteen seconds flat, the little South American was completely naked and was in one of the bathrooms, trying out the shower. Anthony walked over to the telephone by the side of the bed and, after searching around in the recesses of his memory for a moment, he dialled a number.

"Gordon? This is Anthony Bridges."

"Hello, Mr. Bridges. Long time no see." The voice at the other end was very husky. Anthony used to think it had been caused by the owner having his throat cut at some time or another; it was only after knowing Gordon for six months that he had discovered that his supposition was correct. When Anthony had been with the BBC working on documentary films, he and a film unit had spent three weeks in the East End of London filming a programme about the local drug scene. Gordon had attached himself to the unit as a sort of unofficial guide and interpreter. Half way through the filming Gordon had been picked up by the police for breaking and entering; Anthony had provided him with what he had not realised at the time was an entirely false alibi, and Gordon had been set free. His gratitude had been completely out of proportion to the effort Anthony had expended; he had even tried to split the loot from the job with Anthony on a fifty-fifty basis. Anthony, who had genuinely believed in Gordon's innocence, had declined as politely as he could. Gordon had told him that any time he needed a favour, somebody duffing up, a boot put in here or there, a quick abortion, a supply of pills or pot, then Anthony was to let him know. The last time Anthony had called him had been six months ago when he had lost his front door keys. Gordon had appeared on the scene looking impossibly villainish, opened the door in two seconds with a visiting card, and disappeared just as quickly with a finger to his lips and a "Mum's the word". He had even called Anthony the following day to ask him if he needed a good outlet for the loot. Anthony had finally convinced him that it *was* his house, and that was the last time he had spoken to Gordon.

"What can I do for you, Mr. Bridges?" croaked Gordon from the other end of the line.

"I . . . I need some whores," said Anthony.

"How many?" Anthony glanced towards the bathroom where the noise of the shower was mingled with Ramirez's surprisingly powerful baritone voice.

"One, I suppose," said Anthony. "But I need two or three for selection."

"Not like you, Mr. Bridges. Not like you at all."

"They're not for me," said Anthony in quiet anguish. "They're for a business associate."

"If you say so, Mr. Bridges. Go down to the Babette Club, in Greek Street. Ask for Mario. Tell him I sent you. He'll fix you up."

"Will he know what I want?"

"I'll call him right now. Don't forget – the Babette Club."

"Thank you, Gordon."

"Think nothing of it, Mr. Bridges. Happy to oblige. Have a good time!" And the phone went dead, just as Ramirez, naked and dripping, came from the bathroom.

"I am being ten minutes Mr. Bridges, no longer." Anthony nodded and started towards the living room. "No, please. Stay and talking to me please."

Anthony sat down on the edge of the bed and tried not to look at Ramirez. He hated to be in the company of a naked person of the same sex; it embarrased him. He would happily spend days and nights stark naked with any woman he was

65

dating, but some throwback to his boarding school days when, along with a hundred other boys, he would be herded into cold showers and communal changing rooms, had instilled in him a hearty, healthy dislike for the male unclothed body when it wasn't his own. So he stared pointedly at an opulent Rubens type nude on the wall opposite him, wondering what he was possibly going to talk about.

"How is the weather at home?" he asked finally.

Ramirez had opened his brief case and now took out a small, portable iron. He plugged it in and began pressing his trousers on the dressing table. He looked round at Anthony.

"The weather?"

"At home?"

"I am sorry, Mr. Bridges. This is some sort of a code, no?"

"No," said Anthony, wishing that he had never started. "I just wondered how the weather was where you came from."

"The sun shines, or it does not. It rains, or it does not rain. Sometimes it is hot, sometimes cold. The weather in my country is the same as the weather everywhere else," said Ramirez. He looked at Anthony for a brief moment, then with a small shrug, he spat on the iron and continued to press his pants.

"Interesting," said Anthony. Then, because he couldn't think of anything else to say, he continued, hating himself for doing so. "It's the same here," he said.

"What is the same?"

"The weather."

Ramirez nodded a couple of times, slowly. "Ah, yes," he said. Then, satisfied with the crease in his trousers, he pulled them on and zipped them up. There was one clean shirt in his brief case. He unwrapped it from its laundry wrappings, climbed into it, and a minute later he was ready. "We go now," he said.

Vastly relieved, Anthony got to his feet and they both headed out of the bedroom.

"The Babette Club," said Anthony to the chauffeur. "It's in Greek Street."

"Yes, sir," said the chauffeur impassively, as the two men climbed into the back of the car. For a few moments there was silence, then Ramirez brought something up tentatively.

'Mr. Bridges. I am not wanting you to think that I have a big hunger for money, which I most certainly do, but ever before when I am visiting your country on business your company is supplying to me a small spending money."

Anthony was all apologies. "My God, I forgot! I'm terribly sorry." He pulled out the five hundred pounds Walpole had given him. "I was supposed to have given you this when you got off the aeroplane."

Ramirez smiled and put the money in an inside pocket without even looking at it. "Thank you. Now I am feeling better. Tell me, Mr. Bridges, the whores, what are they like?"

Anthony shrugged. "You know whores," he said.

"Sí, I know whores," said Ramirez with a chuckle.

*   *   *

The Babette Club was like any other hardcore nightclub in London; dark, quite large, and invariably half empty. With the prices they charged it was only necessary to fill the place to fifteen per cent of capacity to break even. Going down the stairs, Anthony stumbled in the half light, but Ramirez steadied him. "I am seeing very well in the dark," he said. It's just as well, thought Anthony, who was having trouble telling the sex of the people down here, let alone whether they were pretty or not. Out of the thirty-odd tables in the place, fourteen were occupied exclusively by girls. As far as he could see, only two tables held paying customers, and at one of those an argument was going on as to the amount of the bill. A rather dispirited four-piece band was thrumming away in one corner, to the enjoyment of absolutely nobody.

Anthony asked the waiter who showed them to their table if he would be kind enough to fetch Mario. "Tell him I'm a friend of Gordon's," he added.

Another waiter appeared and asked them what they would like to drink.

"Scottish whisky, please," said Ramirez.

"Same for me," said Anthony. "With soda."

A bowl of ice appeared, a virgin bottle of scotch, half a dozen sodas, a girl to take their photograph and another to sell them cigarettes. Then the girls were hustled away as Mario arrived. He was short, round and Spanish. Ramirez recognised this almost immediately and the two of them started to gabble away in their native tongue. That's a relief, thought Anthony. At least he will be able to ask for his own whores. He poured himself a drink and looked around.

Now that his eyes were becoming accustomed to the dark, he was able to recognise that some of the girls weren't at all bad looking. And they were all staring straight at him, all thirty-two of them; some of them subtly, some boldly, some winking, some smiling, some scowling. There were white girls, black girls, blondes, brunettes, tall girls, short girls, fat girls, thin girls. Anthony lowered his gaze towards his drink and fixed it there. He felt like a man at an auction sale; one false move, a nod, a wink or a cough, and it would be "sold to the embarrased gentleman in the corner". He risked a sideways glance at Ramirez. He was explaining something to

68

Mario, who was nodding vigorously, understanding and apparently heartily approving of everything that was being said. Then he said something further to Ramirez, glancing at Anthony as he did so. Ramirez nodded his head and said something else. Mario smiled and disappeared.

"Everything all right?" asked Anthony hopefully.

"Everything is very good. He is *mucho sympatico* that *hombre.*"

"I'm glad," said Anthony. He downed his drink. "Now if you will excuse me, I . . ."

"Where are you going?"

Anthony stopped, half in, half out of his chair. "Home," he lied.

"Home? Home to where?" Then he smiled. "Of course, you are going back to the apartment. You are trusting Carlos Ramirez to pick your whores for you."

Anthony sat down again. "I say . . ." he said. "I mean, I don't particularly *want* a whore. Not that I've got anything against them, of course." In fact Anthony had never paid for a woman in his life, and it wasn't only because he had never had the money. He felt that to pay for sex wasn't quite right, a sort of denial of one's own virility.

"You do not expect me to spend the night by myself?" asked Ramirez. He wasn't smiling any longer.

"Not completely," said Anthony. "That's why we're here, isn't it?"

"We are here to find our companions for the night. Two for you and two for me."

"I say . . ." said Anthony. But for the life of him, he couldn't think what it was he wanted to say. Then it didn't matter any longer, because Mario reappeared with four girls in tow. He introduced them by their christian names.

69

"This is Beth, and Eleanor, and Brigitte and Shirleen." It couldn't be, thought Anthony; but it was; it was Daddy's sexatary. She squealed with delight when she recognised him. "Henry," she said. "How groovy to see you again."

"It's Anthony."

"Sorry," she said, as she plonked herself down next to him. "I'm terrible with names." Then she tucked her arm beneath his in a proprietorial fashion and beamed around the table as the other girls sorted themselves out. Beth was a big-boned blonde with a sullen mouth and a predatory gleam in her eye; Eleanor was as black as the ace of spades and extremely attractive; Brigitte was a pale little thing who looked like an undernourished fourteen year old. Four bottles of champagne appeared, as did half a dozen menus. The cigarette girl reappeared; so did the photographer and another girl Anthony hadn't seen before who was selling boxes of chocolates and teddy bears. The evening got under way.

*   *   *

Between the caviar and the *filet mignon,* Anthony asked Shirleen to dance. He was strictly a frug and shuffle man, but he wanted to talk to her out of range of the others.

"What are you doing here?" was his first question.

"The same as you, I suppose, darling. Actually it's my first week here. Mr. Henshawe fired me last Thursday."

"Couldn't you get another job as a secretary?"

"Well, it's a bit difficult really. You see I can't do shorthand, or typing, or filing, or any of those things. So I thought I had better try for the thing I do best."

"I see."

She moved in closer, so that all her visible and invisible assets were tightly pressed against him, and nibbled at his

70

ear. "It's wonderful to see you again . . . Couldn't we give the others the slip and go off on our own? I'm not honestly mad for mixed doubles, are you?"

"I've never tried them," admitted Anthony. "What happens?"

"Oh, you know . . . variations and permutations and exhibitions and all that. It's very boring. I'm a one-man girl myself."

"That's funny," said Anthony. "I'm a one-girl man. He thought hard for a moment or two and then produced a plan. "Look, its a bit difficult. Señor Ramirez is an important client of ours and I can't very well ditch him just like that. But when we get to the apartment, you pretend you feel very sick and I'll tell him I'm going to drive you home and come back with a replacement. Only I won't, of course . . . go back I mean. How's that?"

"Groovy!"

"You think you can act sick?"

"I'll just look at that horrid little man and I'll *feel* sick."

*   *   *

It worked like a charm.

When the Rolls drew up outside the apartment and the rest of the girls began to tumble out, chattering and giggling like a flock of starlings, Shirleen remained huddled in the far corner of the back seat, her hands clasped over her abdomen and her eyes closed.

Anthony put his head in at the door. "Are you all right?" he asked.

"I feel terribly sick."

"Come in and have a drink and you'll feel better," he said extra loudly for Carlos' benefit.

71

Shirleen shook her head and put her hand firmly over her mouth.

"Do you really feel ill?" Anthony asked.

Shirleen nodded miserably. Anthony turned to Ramirez, who was getting impatient. "It's no good. She isn't going to be any use to us," he said. "Tell you what – I'll drop her at the club and bring back a replacement. Can you manage the other three while I'm gone?"

"I am managing very well, thank you," boasted Ramirez. "Maybe you should be bringing two replacements, no?" He dug an elbow in Anthony's ribs and shepherded the girls into the apartment.

Anthony got back into the Rolls. Shirleen was still putting on an Oscar-winning performance.

"Where to?" he asked, quietly.

"You want to go to your place, or mine?"

"Where's yours?"

"Hill Street."

"Let's go there. It's close enough that I can walk back."

*   *   *

It was quite a while before Anthony walked back. In fact, a muddy grey dawn was breaking over Hyde Park as he crossed Curzon Street and turned into Shepherd's Market.

He had left behind him a soft, warm, sleepy Shirleen and he was missing her already. In the last five hours he had learned a great deal about her – and he liked what he had learned.

He had quickly found out that she could give Lilian a head and a half start in athleticism and still leave her standing. She made love as though she had been starved for months and he was her first square meal since Christmas.

72

But she also measured up in a hundred other ways to the dream woman he had always promised himself. Her lips were, as his dream had stipulated, like pale velvet, and her voice like melting honey. After the first wild explosion, they spent long hours gazing into each other's eyes, holding hands and making soft, gentle love. He even fell asleep with his head between her breasts.

But the most unexpected moment came when he woke up, looked sleepily at his watch, and announced that it was time for him to leave. Shirleen clung to him and begged him not to go. They made love again, briefly but beautifully. And then, when he was dressed and ready to leave, he rather awkwardly produced his wallet, counted out some fivers and handed them to her.

Immediately she brushed them aside and he was amazed to see tears in her eyes. "How could you!" she said. "You don't think I made love to you for money, do you?"

"But you missed out on the party. You'd have been paid for that."

"That's different. For that you couldn't pay me enough. But tonight was on the house. I happen to think you're rather groovy."

As he entered the foyer of the Shepherd's Market apartment block and went inside, Anthony could still hear the exact tone of her voice as she said it, could still feel the velvet of her lips as she clung to him afterwards. But these thoughts were quickly dispersed as he felt a nudge behind him, and turning he saw a young man standing close to him. "About bloody time," said the young man.

Anthony said nothing.

"Well open the fucking door and let's go inside," said the young man. Anthony did as he was told. Any desire to argue

73

was dispelled by the fact that the young man was holding a bloody great rifle pointing straight at his navel.

* * *

"Charlie Whitehead," said the young man, as he pushed Anthony into the apartment. Anthony vaguely heard him, but couldn't take his eyes off the gun. The opening at the end looked as large as the Blackwall tunnel. Slowly he pulled himself together.

"No," he said.

"No what?" asked the young man.

"I'm not Mr. Whitehead. My name is Bridges."

"I know that," said the young man. "*I'm* Charlie White-head."

"How do you do?" said Anthony. It was the best he could manage.

"Where's Ramirez?"

"Anthony nodded towards one of the bedrooms. "In there, I expect."

"Let's fetch him," said Charlie. "I want to get this over."

"Yes, sir,' said Anthony, wondering whether there was anything he could do to warn Carlos what was waiting for him. Already he could see his lovely new job going out of the window. He could almost hear Walpole. "I put the man in your charge and you allow him to get shot." Then the further implication hit him—if Ramirez was going to be shot, then he, as witness to the deed, would probably be going the same way; to say nothing of the three girls who would also have to be silenced. He could see the headlines now. "Massacre in West End love nest." My God, the newspapers would have fun with that one. Panic stricken now, he turned back to face Charlie, who screwed up his eyes and frowned at him.

74

"What's the matter with you? You look as though you've been out on the tiles all night."

"I have."

"Never mind," said Charlie. "It'll all be over soon. Just get Randy Ramirez out here."

"Do you mind if I have a quick drink first?" asked Anthony. "I need it."

"Make it fast then."

"One for you?"

"All right. Just a small scotch."

It was then that Anthony, whose brain had been working overtime like a crazed computer, did something very foolish. He had always considered himself a coward; if a man started an argument in a bar, he would tip his hat politely and change his bar; if a couple of louts were pushing people off the pavement, he would cross to the other side of the road before he reached them; and if a drunk insulted his girl-friend, he would tell the girl to shut up and mind her own business. But whether it was *après sex* euphoria because of his newly discovered passion for Shirleen, or the onset of his hangover, he reacted as he had never done before—suddenly and violently.

As Charlie took the scotch he held out to him, the barrel of the rifle was automatically lowered towards the floor, so that for the first time it was not pointing directly at Anthony's crotch. Anthony stepped forward and threw the contents of his glass straight towards Charlie's face; at the same time making a diving grab for the rifle barrel. He missed the rifle completely and fell flat on his face on the floor. This is it, he decided. Please make it quick and aim carefully, as I don't want to suffer unduly. He lay with his face pressed into the carpet waiting for the impact of the bullet to smash him into oblivion.

"What are you?" said Charlie from somewhere above him. "Some kind of a nut or something." Anthony risked a quick look. The rifle lay on the floor beside him and Charlie was mopping himself down with a handkerchief. Apparently the scotch had missed his face and spilled all down the front of his suit; and he was livid.

"Jesus Christ," he muttered. "What sort of kooks have we got working for us these days?" He looked down at Anthony. "Are you on a trip or something?"

Anthony answered him without moving. "I thought you were going to shoot me."

"You thought what?"

"You were pointing that gun at me."

"I wasn't pointing at you. I was just holding it."

"I didn't know that."

"Why the hell would I point a gun at you?"

"The thought crossed my mind, too," said Anthony, easing himself up on to his elbows.

"For Christ's sake get up and pull yourself together!"

Anthony started to sit up. "What did you say your name was?" he asked.

"Charlie Whitehead."

"How do you do? I'm Anthony Bridges." He reached up his hand and Charlie shook it, at the same time dragging him to his feet.

"I know who you are," said Charlie. "Now let's get Ramirez out here. Then we can all go home."

"Yes, sir," said Anthony.

"And stop calling me 'sir'. We both work for the same firm."

76

"We do?"

Charlie raised his eyes to heaven. Then he decided that if anything was going to get done he was going to have to do it himself. "Which bedroom is he in?"

"Over there," said Anthony. He watched while Charlie walked over and opened the door. The lights were off in the bedroom but Charlie turned them on and shouted: "Come on, Carlos! Get your grubby little South American ass out here!"

Anthony heard a groan from one of the girls and a moment later the naked figure of Carlos bounced out of the bedroom, throwing his arms round Charlie's neck. "Sharlie! It is good to be seeing you, Sharlie."

Charlie pushed him away. "Jesus! You'd better put some clothes on, or Tony will be getting the wrong idea."

"Wait, Sharlie. Two minutes I put clothes on." Carlos went back into the bedroom, to reappear wearing a sheet draped around him like a toga. Watched by Charlie he picked up the rifle and started slamming the bolt in and out rapidly; then as Anthony moved towards the bar, he threw the rifle to his shoulder aiming it straight between Anthony's eyes. Involuntarily Anthony threw his hands into the air, but Carlos had already lowered the rifle once more and was hefting it in his hands.

"Is old gun, Sharlie," he said. It was a short magazine Lee Enfield, the rifle so beloved by the British army between the wars and during most of World War Two.

"It's not an AR 10 or any of those other fancy new automatic weapons," said Charlie. "But it's what you can afford."

Carlos shook his head. "Not me, Sharlie. Not my money."

"Then what are you worried about?"

77

"I have reputation to look after," said Carlos. "I am big man where I come from."

"Come off it, Carlos. You only just got out of the pokey."

"I know it, Sharlie. But I am still big man. I tell you what I do. For this old, old gun, I give you twenty American dollars."

"Twenty-five," said Charlie.

"Twenty-one. Higher than that and I go broken."

"Twenty-three. I'll be skinned alive if I sell for less."

Anthony was fascinated. Here was a man calling round at six o'clock in the morning to sell a twenty-five dollar rifle to another man who had five hundred pounds cash in his pocket; and they were arguing about a few measly cents. He studied Charlie during the negotiations, seeing him clearly for the first time. He was about twenty-seven or eight years old, neat and anonymous looking. He wore his hair cut short, and his clothes looked as though they had been bought in America. He had a nervous habit of tugging at his right earlobe with his left hand, but apart from that he seemed perfectly in control of the situation; always discounting the idiocy of the whole scene.

The price fluctuated between twenty-one dollars and fifty cents and twenty-two dollars and fifty cents, with Charlie praising the virtues of the rifle and Carlos saying he wouldn't let his worst enemy load this gun and fire it in case it blew up in his face. Eventually they settled for twenty-two dollars even.

"Ammunition?" asked Carlos.

"Seven dollars a hundred," said Charlie. Carlos offered three dollars and finally they agreed on five. The two men shook hands and business seemed to be over for the night.

78

"You excuse me one minute," said Carlos, urgently. "I must go to the toilet."

When he had disappeared at the double, Charlie looked anxiously at Anthony. "You been out in the field yet?" he asked.

"Which field?"

"Have you done any selling or buying?"

"No."

"Well, that's how it's done."

"It seems an awful lot of trouble to go through for the sake of a couple of dollars."

"Those two dollars make the difference between a good deal and an extra good deal. I just made an extra good deal."

"That's nice," said Anthony.

"Ten thousand rifles at twenty-two dollars each and one million rounds of ammo at five dollars per hundred. That comes to two hundred and seventy thousand dollars. I would have been happy with two hundred and thirty thousand and Carlos would have paid three hundred thousand. This way we're both satisfied and we'll do business again."

"Two hundred and seventy thousand dollars!" said Anthony.

"That's it," said Charlie. "My one per cent commission comes to two thousand seven hundred."

"You just sold him ten thousand rifles?"

"And a million rounds to shoot from the bloody things."

"To Carlos Ramirez?"

Charlie looked at Anthony for a moment. "Are you okay?" he asked.

"I'm fine, thank you," said Anthony.

"In that case, I'll go and get cleaned up." He surveyed his

stained suit and clucked his tongue. "I've got a plane to catch at ten o'clock."

He tossed the gun on to the settee and strode into one of the bedrooms. Within a few moments, excited female squeals suggested that, whatever he was doing, it wasn't just washing.

Anthony moved over to the bar and poured himself another drink. So at last he knew the business he was in. He hadn't even been aware until now that the buying and selling of guns went on outside of governments. Now it seemed that it did, and that he was a part of it. What's more, he had just seen Charlie make two thousand seven hundred dollars in ten minutes. He couldn't for the life of him think what Carlos Ramirez was going to do with ten thousand rifles and a million rounds of ammunition. He resolved to ask Charlie, but then he changed his mind. He'd made enough of a twit out of himself for one night. He poured himself another drink and began to savour again the one thing that had gone well— in a tiny apartment in Hill Street.

4

LAMBOOLA WAS THE HOTTEST, THE DIRTIEST, THE nastiest place that Anthony had ever dreamed of. If it was a typical example of what was being given back to the Africans, it was a wonder the whole continent hadn't been handed back a hundred years ago. He had been there two days now and already he had developed prickly heat and raging diarrhoea; added to this he was covered with bites from the assortment of insects that infested his hotel room; he had a permanent, constant headache and he couldn't sleep.

It seemed there was only one doctor who knew what he was talking about in Manville, the capital city, and Anthony had gone to see him an hour after stepping off the aeroplane.

Doctor Ondoma was huge, black and shiny; he laughed at everything that appeared before him, be it a multiple fracture with complications or a sick headache. Physical pain and illness were his business, and he enjoyed it like nobody had before him. So amusing did the good doctor find it, and so infectious was his amusement, that Anthony, who had been feeling just about as low as was possible, even found himself grinning at his own misery. Ondoma had pumped him full of penicillin and given him some tablets to take and some ointment to rub on his bites. Nevertheless, on the morning of the third day, Anthony lay in his room wondering whether he could possibly last another twenty-four hours, and even if he wanted to.

*   *   *

"You will fly to Manville on Wednesday," Walpole had said. It was the day after Carlos Ramirez had left. While Charlie was still cavorting in the shower to the accompaniment of shrill feminine screams, Carlos had informed Anthony that he wanted to catch the afternoon flight to Rio. In the meantime he was going shopping to Saville Road and Marks and Spencers. And please, as he needed to buy some clothes, would Anthony pay off the young ladies?

"How much?" he enquired.

"Three hundred pounds," Ramirez told him.

At first Anthony couldn't believe he had heard correctly. "Three hundred," he exclaimed. "For one night?" Ramirez dug an elbow in his ribs. "Ah! But what a night!"

Anthony suddenly realised he hadn't got that much money left. But the girls, having had their fun with Charlie, had decided to go back to bed and he was able to go down to the bank when it opened at ten and cash a cheque. He paid off the girls, when they left at noon, promising to see them again at the first opportunity; then he ordered the car, picked up Carlos and drove him to the airport. Carlos had bought so many clothes that his baggage was now considerably overweight. Anthony paid for this with another cheque and then tried not to look embarrassed as Carlos threw his arms round his neck and kissed him on both cheeks.

"*Adios*, Antonio, my old, old friend! I am having the most best time and I am doing good business. When you come to South America, I am showing you the same – good business and bad girls!" He was speaking very loudly and Anthony started to curl with embarrassment. But then a swift pat on the back and Carlos disappeared. Anthony took the car back to the Manchip Hotel and spent the rest of the day filling in his expense vouchers and wondering how one indented for three whores at a hundred pounds each without it looking too indelicate.

*   *   *

The evening he had spent with Shirleen, which proved so satisfactory that somehow "evening" had extended until ten o'clock next morning. As he entered his hotel room, the telephone was ringing. It was Miss Cremin.

"I had to ring three times," she snapped. "Lunch. Twelve-thirty."

Once again he found himself facing Walpole across the salt beef sandwiches. It was then that Walpole told him he would be flying to Lamboola that evening.

"Yes, sir," said Anthony and sat waiting.

"Well?"

"What do I do when I get there?"

"You'll be met," said Walpole. "Carter will meet you."

83

He had put in his expense account to Millwright, who paid it without batting an eyelid; he had been handed a first-class one way aeroplane ticket and another two hundred and fifty pounds, and he had gone back to the Manchip to pack.

*   *   *

His one worry was that he couldn't let Shirleen know he was leaving. Her phone didn't answer and, when he took a taxi around to Hill Street, there was no reply to her doorbell either. Eventually he left a note in her letterbox and rushed to the airport.

Oddly enough, he was more worried about her than he was when he found there was no Carter to meet him at the airport. He took a taxi to the only hotel in town, the Layfayette; he located Doctor Ondoma through the hotel, and since then he had spent his time shuffling between the hotel and the doctor's office in a miasma of misery and discomfort. Occasionally he would wonder about Carter and whether he ought to make some effort to contact the man, but then he would have to go racing to the toilet, and in the half an hour that followed he invariably forgot all about Carter, his reason for being here, and everything else save the agonising cramps in his stomach, the constant irritation of his prickly heat, and the itch of his bites. When, on the third day, a man suddenly appeared in his hotel room, Anthony had absolutely no idea who he was and couldn't have cared less.

"Bridges?" barked the man. Anthony, who had been dozing between visits to the toilet, looked at him, bleary-eyed.

"Yes, I'm Bridges," he admitted.

"Carter," said the man, clicking his heels together. Anthony forced himself up on to one elbow and looked at his visitor more closely. Carter was six feet tall, straight as a

84

ramrod and immaculate. His khaki drill shirt was pressed in knife-edged creases, as were his riding breeches which were tucked into a pair of riding boots which dazzled with their shine. He wore a Sam Browne type belt and carried an elaborate flywhisk as though it were an officer's cane. His hair was sandy coloured and close cropped, his eyes blue and cold, his mouth hard and his skin weatherbeaten. He looked every inch a soldier, which he couldn't have been because there were no white soldiers in Lamboola.

"Sorry I didn't meet you," said Carter. "Up country." Anthony subsided on to the pillow once more. "Under the weather?" asked Carter, still standing just inside the door.

"You could say that."

"Happens to everyone. Don't drink the water, eat everything out of tins, and take plenty of booze; it poisons the insects. Seen the M.O.?" Anthony nodded. "Which one?"

"The laughing one."

"Ondoma. Not a bad doctor for a wog," said Carter. "Permission to sit?"

"I beg your pardon?"

"Permission to sit down?"

"Go ahead," said Anthony.

Carter pulled up a straight back chair and sat, still ramrod straight, his back not touching the chair. "Ready to start work?" he asked.

"No," said Anthony, without preamble.

"Sorry. Got to! Boat arrives tomorrow at oh four hundred. Want to start loading right away."

"Go ahead," said Anthony. "Don't let me stop you."

"Can't do that," said Carter. "You've got to check the manifests. If you're short the other end you'll blame us. Can't have that."

"You check them," said Anthony, with no idea what either of them was talking about.

"You trust me?" said Carter.

"Implicitly."

There was a moment's pause and then Carter cleared his throat awkwardly. "Damned decent of you," he said. "Damned decent."

"Pleasure."

"Nobody has ever trusted me like that before."

"Mmm," said Anthony, who had nearly stopped listening.

"Bloody gratifying, if you must know."

"Mmm," said Anthony.

"Damned sporting." Anthony had started to doze off again, but now he jerked awake suddenly as Carter poked him with the handle of his flywhisk. "I like you, Bridges," he said. "You're my kind of person."

"Good," said Anthony.

"Sorry I can't oblige though."

He didn't get through to Anthony who said, "You just go right ahead." as he slid off towards sleep once more.

He received another jab with the flywhisk. "No, old man, you didn't understand me. I said I'm sorry I can't do what you ask. Company regs."

Anthony shifted on to his elbow again. "What is?"

"Every agent is completely responsible for his shipment from the moment it leaves the warehouse until delivery." Something stirred in the recesses of Anthony's mind. Paragraph eight: the party of the second part will take full responsibility for any or all of the consignments in his charge and will be held financially responsible for their loss or damage howsoever caused . . . up to a value of one million dollars.

86

"What shipment?" he asked.

"Your shipment. Ten thousand SMLE's and one million rounds of ammo for same."

"*My* shipment?"

"For delivery to Santhoma."

"Where?"

"Santhoma. It's in South America."

Anthony managed to struggle up to a sitting position. "Are you sure you've got the right Bridges?"

Carter stood up abruptly. "Good man," he said. "Sense of humour and all that. I'll pick you up in one hour."

He clicked his heels again and only just refrained from saluting, turning the gesture into a sort of casual wave. A moment later, he was gone. Anthony looked at the door as it closed behind him. He was still looking at it two minutes later when his stomach started to knot once more. He tottered out of bed and just made it along the passage in time. Ten minutes later he was back in his room, his mind made up. He pushed the bell beside his bed, and when the waiter appeared he ordered a bottle of scotch. He had to have a drink. Without one he wasn't going to be able to stay on his feet, let alone meet Carter one hour from now.

Carter picked him up exactly one hour later outside the hotel. He was driving a jeep and he didn't bother to get out. He drew up in a cloud of dust. "Hop in!" he said. Anthony climbed in and they were off in another cloud of dust. With four very large scotches inside him. Anthony had to admit to feeling a little better; there had been no stomach cramps for an hour, his bites didn't itch as much as they had, and even his headache had retreated to the back of his skull, where it still lurked, but without the same devastating effect. As they drove, Anthony looked around him, seeing Manville properly for the first time. He found it as depressing as his original impressions had led him to believe; no building higher than three floors and most of them looking as though they had been made out of dirty mud. There was one construction project about half a mile from the hotel which seemed as though it might have amounted to something, but obviously the money had run out just before the second floor; and while the scaffolding optimistically towered fifty feet above that point, there was nothing between except empty space.

"Know anything about Lamboola?" asked Carter. Anthony shook his head and Carter proceeded to give him a potted history of the place. Until ten years before, it had belonged to the French, but even they hadn't thought much of it. There were no minerals to exploit and, since the abolition of the slave trade, it had been good for absolutely nothing. Unlike most of their colonial possessions, they had put very little money and practically no time or effort into Lamboola. Then a minor politician who had just come back from a visit to Kenya made the mistake of saying that Lamboola should overthrow the yoke of French Imperialism and become independent. France seized this opportunity and couldn't get out of the place fast enough. Their departure left a vacuum in what had been a pretty airless place from the start. The Russians, the Chinese and the Americans were too busy exploiting the rest of Africa to bother, so the country had limped on since then in exactly the same way it had been doing for the past five hundred years. The people were cheerful, feckless, completely unreliable and bone idle. Give them a cow and a potato patch and they were content. The climate was impossible, trade non-existent, industry minimal and even then strictly for home consumption. Politicians

88

were indifferent rather than corrupt; the crime rate was unbelievably low mainly because nobody could be bothered, and education consisted in making sure everyone could count to ten before they were sixteen years old.

"So why are we here?" asked Anthony.

"Taxes," said Carter.

"What about them?"

"There aren't any."

"And?"

"We employ about fifty people . . . when they bother to turn up. That makes us the largest employer in the whole country. So we get to write our own laws when necessary."

"Paragraph fifteen," said Anthony.

"What?"

"Any dispute under this contract shall be settled under the laws of Lamboola."

"Sorry, old man, don't get it."

"As the largest employer in the country, I suppose you get to run the courts as well."

"More or less. There's only one judge in the place, and he's on a retainer to the company."

"Convenient."

Carter chuckled. "It certainly is."

There was silence between them for the next couple of miles. Carter drove the same way that he looked, with a military precision and Anthony found himself wondering about him.

"You live out here permanently?" he asked.

"Been here two years now. One more to go on this contract. Then I'll probably sign on for another three."

"You run the company here, do you?"

"Quartermaster. Always been a quartermaster. Quartermaster in the army before I joined the company. Good job; everything neat and orderly; everything listed in triplicate; know where you are all the time."

"I was in the army," said Anthony, without quite knowing why.

"Good life the army," said Carter. "Wish I'd stayed in."

"Why didn't you?"

"Couldn't. They slung me out."

"Oh," said Anthony, wishing he hadn't asked. But Carter didn't seem to mind.

"I was mess officer; they caught me with my fingers in the till."

"Oh," said Anthony again.

"Innocent, of course," said Carter. "I had my fingers in the till certainly, but it wasn't for my own benefit. I wanted to buy some special wines for the mess, a bargain. The committee wouldn't sanction it. Can't resist a bargain though, never could. So I milked the mess funds and then the bastard who was selling me the wine made off with the loot and the wine as well. They ran an audit before I had time to make good the loss. Messy business. Court martial and all that. Came to work for the company just after that. They needed a quartermaster, and that's what they got ... Here we are,"

Anthony looked up as the jeep swung off the dirt road and into a compound. They were about five miles out of town and, as far as Anthony could make out, slap in the middle of nowhere. As far as the eye could see in every direction stretched depressing looking scrubland; and placed in the centre, for no apparent reason, was the compound. There were three very large warehouses, dilapidated buildings with dried mud walls and corrugated iron roofs; there were three

90

or four smaller buildings, obviously offices of some sort, and that was all. The area was surrounded by a high wire fence which at one time may have served to keep people in or out; but that time must have been long past because the wire had rusted away or broken in a number of places, leaving gaps large enough to drive a truck through.

Carter pulled up the jeep outside one of the smaller buildings. "Just go and check we've still got a staff; then I'll show you around," he said.

He disappeared into the building and Anthony climbed out of the jeep and stood looking around. Behind one of the warehouses were parked a dozen large army trucks; a few Africans were pottering around beneath the bonnets, while others were just sitting in the sun doing nothing. Now that the jeep had stopped Anthony realised just how hot the sun was. It still needed an hour to noon, but the heat was almost suffocating.

In a few moments Carter reappeared. "Ready for the guided tour?"

Anthony decided he felt as ready as he would ever be, and started after Carter across the compound to the nearest of the warehouses. The large double doors at the end were open and Carter walked in.

"This is where we keep the heavy stuff," he said. "Not the artillery; that's up country in our number two depot. Here we have the light anti-tank weapons, bazookas, heavy machine guns, mortars, stuff like that."

The warehouse appeared larger from the inside than it did from outside. Once his eyes had got used to the change from the dazzling sunlight outside, Anthony could make out that the place was crammed to the rafters with large wooden crates. After a moment he could see that they were laid out

91

neatly in well regulated rows, forming their own passage-ways between. He followed Carter along the centre aisle as Carter gave a commentary, reading from the cryptic notations stencilled on the sides of the crates.

"Bought this lot from the Moroccans last year. Lovely shooter. One-fifty rounds per minute. Doesn't work too well in the cold though. Sold a couple of dozen to a Finnish outfit. Right in the middle of a scrap everything seized up in the frost. Pity about that; they were good customers. Here's a beauty . . . a bazooka the Americans developed for Korea. It delivers an armour-piercing shell that can crack open a tank like a tin of sardines. Sold a couple to some shady looking customers from Florida last year; said they were in the banking business. Those over there are good old Bren guns, ex-British army. Don't know why they ever got rid of them. Lovely shooter! Those mortars over there will drop a shell on a sixpence from a mile away if you know how to handle them."

"Very useful," said Anthony, who felt that some comment was called for. They had reached the far end of the ware-house by now. Carter opened a door and stood back for Anthony to go through. He did so, finding himself in the blinding light of the compound once again.

"Your consignment is in number two warehouse. You can start checking it later," said Carter. "Want to see the ammo store?"

Anthony didn't, but he didn't dare say so. He followed Carter over to the second warehouse. Inside it looked exactly the same; a series of wooden crates piled to the roof. Here, too, Carter gave him the tour; anti-tank shells, mortar bombs, rifle and pistol ammunition; tracers, nickel-coated, soft-nosed, high velocity, low impediment; whatever the gun, Carter had

92

the wherewithal to provide for it, all neatly arranged and to hand. A group of Africans was lazily stacking some crates. Carter walked over to them and said something in the impossible language of the country. One of the Africans grinned and, levering the lid off one of the crates, he delved inside. He pulled something out and handed it to Carter. Carter turned suddenly and threw it to Anthony.

"Catch!" he said. With reflexes conditioned on countless schoolboy cricket fields, Anthony caught. He looked at it and promptly dropped it. It was a hand grenade. The Africans hooted with laughter and even Carter grinned.

"Works every time," he said. "Little joke of mine."

"Very amusing," said Anthony, dragging his tattered nerves together. "But isn't it a little dangerous?"

Carter picked up the grenade and started tossing it casually from hand to hand. "Safe as the Rock of Gibraltar until the pin's out," he said. "Drive a truck over it and nothing would happen. But you knew that, surely?" His amused expression became tinged with a certain amount of concern. "Didn't you?"

"Not really," said Anthony.

"You were in the army, you said."

"I was away sick the day they did grenades."

Carter threw the grenade back to the African who caught it neatly and dropped it back in its box. "What do you know about the short magazine Lee Enfield?" he asked, starting towards the doors of the warehouse.

"Not much," said Anthony, falling into step beside him. "Bit before my time."

"You have fired one though?"

"Not actually."

"Then how are you going to demonstrate it?"

93

"I didn't know I was."

They were out in the sunlight once more, heading across towards the building that held Carter's office. But now Carter stopped and turned to him.

"Don't think I'm being nosy old chap, but what *did* they tell you in London?"

"Nothing."

"Nothing?"

"Nothing."

"They must have told you *something*."

"Not really. They gave me an aeroplane ticket and told me that you'd meet me."

"Nothing else?"

Anthony shook his head, wishing he could be more helpful.

Carter looked at him for a moment. "Come on, old man," he said finally. "You and I have got some talking to do."

*　　*　　*

Anthony followed him to his office, through an outer room where two African clerks worked, into the back room. Carter closed the door behind him.

"Sit down," he said. Anthony sat. "Drink?"

Anthony nodded. "Please."

Carter poured a couple of large drinks from a bottle of scotch and splashed soda into them. "Cheers," he said.

"Cheers," replied Anthony. There was no ice and the drinks were very warm.

Carter took a long swallow, then moved round behind his desk and sat down. He looked at Anthony for a moment, managed a half smile that Anthony took to be one of encouragement, then he took another drink. "Nothing?" he said finally.

94

Anthony shook his head. "Sorry," he said.

"Not even about the consignment?"

"Not even that."

"Didn't you ask?"

"As a matter of fact I did a couple of times."

"And?"

Anthony shrugged. "Nobody seemed very forthcoming."

"I suppose you do know who you are working for?"

"Hengun Incorporated."

"That's a help," said Carter, without sarcasm. "And you know what business we're in?"

"We sell guns?"

"Buy and sell. And not just guns. Tanks, armoured cars, artillery, aeroplanes, warships, rockets, missiles; you name it and if it's got a death potential, we're in the market."

"Death potential?"

Carter smiled a little shyly. "That's my own way of grading the materials we deal in. Want to hear about it?"

"Yes, please."

Carter became a little dreamy as he started to discuss his favourite topic. "Take a scale from one to one hundred. That's your death potential scale. At the bottom end, number one, we have the well known 'blunt instrument'. A club, in other words; the first weapon devised by man. Also the least efficient; that's why it is number one on the scale. Next we have the knife, with all its subdivisions; domestic, flick, bayonet, sword, dagger, etcetera, etcetera. A little higher we have the lance and the spear; see where we're getting?"

"No."

"Distance, that's where we're getting. Distance between subject and object. A lance or a spear for stabbing is higher

95

up the scale than a dagger, but lower down than a spear for throwing. Clear?"

"Clear."

"So what's next on the scale?"

Anthony thought about it for a second. "Bow and arrow?"

"Good," said Carter. "Bow and arrow. Then we have crossbow, and already we're up near number eight. The guns start at ten."

"Why?"

"There was an interesting modification to the crossbow that I came across, a sort of automatic crossbow that fired ten bolts very rapidly one after the other. That became number nine."

"I see," said Anthony.

"So now we get on to firearms. We start with the simplest muzzle loading type, and up we go. Your SMLE's are number forty-two."

"Why do you keep calling them *my* SMLE's?"

"We'll talk about that later. Now, what's number one hundred on the scale, eh?"

Anthony thought about it for a moment. "An inter-continental ballistic missile with an atomic warhead."

Carter grinned his triumph. "That's ninety-seven. Ninety-eight is the multiple warhead ICBM. Ninety-nine and one hundred haven't been invented yet. But they will be."

"Hengun doesn't deal in atomic weapons, does it?" asked Anthony nervously.

"'Fraid not," said Carter. "We buy our stuff from governments mostly; surplus to their own needs. No government has found atomic weapons surplus yet. They will though, sooner or later. And when they do, your friendly neighbourhood death pedlar will be on hand to buy them up. Think of that, old man; try to imagine your commission on a high yield fusion device and the wherewithal to deliver it. You could make a couple of million dollars on one sale." He glanced out of the window. "I'll have to build another warehouse out there when that time comes." He sighed, leaning back in his chair. "In the meantime, we'll just have to keep on dealing in what we can get hold of. Like your short magazine Lee Enfields."

"You promised to talk about that," said Anthony.

"What?"

"Why you call them *my* short magazine Lee Enfields."

"They're your consignment. You sold them; you're responsible for their delivery."

"I didn't sell them."

"You didn't? Who did?"

"Charlie Whitchead."

"Oh," said Carter. "That explains it."

"Explains what?"

"Every agent is responsible for the delivery of the goods that he sells."

"So why isn't Charlie delivering them?"

"Didn't you know? He's dead."

"Charlie Whitehead?"

"Charlie Whitehead."

"But I saw him a few days ago. I was with him when he made the sale."

Carter riffled through some teletype messages on his desk, finally extracting one and holding it up. "Seems someone drove a truck over him on the Champs Elysées. Lovely city, Paris. Bit of luck for you, actually. You'll be completing the deal, so you'll get the commission."

"Poor Charlie," said Anthony, genuinely upset.

Carter shrugged. "It was inevitable."

"I don't see how being killed in a street accident can be inevitable," said Anthony.

"Oh, it wasn't an accident," said Carter. "Definitely not an accident."

"How do you know?"

"The truck drove over him, then reversed and did it all over again."

"On the Champs Elysées?"

"Four o'clock in the morning. Not many people about," said Carter, pushing the teletype message back into the pile. "I must admit, though, I didn't think they would get Charlie so easily. Bright lad, Charlie."

"Who are 'They'?"

"They; Them. The customers."

"Why should the customers want to kill Charlie?"

"The customers always want to kill the supplier. Didn't they tell you that, either?"

"No, they didn't."

"Look at it from the customer's point of view. He buys a few thousand rifles and machine guns and the ammunition necessary to use them. Now what does he want them for?"

"I haven't the faintest idea."

"Revolution, of course. He wants to topple his local government. He buys the guns from Charlie, mounts the revolution, and suddenly *he* is the government. Now he knows how he got where he is, and he knows that there are a lot of other people milling around who would like to do the same thing. But they'll need guns to do it and the chances are that they'll go to Charlie to get them. So let's get rid of Charlie. Lesson number one: never turn your back on a satisfied client."

98

Anthony sat silent for a while, his drink untouched in his hand. Carter took pity on him after a minute.

"Cheer up," he said. "It's not as bad as all that."

"It isn't?"

"Look at the credit side. You're earning good money; all your expenses are paid and you've just made two thousand seven hundred dollars commission."

"So did Charlie."

Carter shrugged. "Perhaps he just got careless. He'd been at it a long time, you know."

"How long?"

"Two years. I remember the first time he came through here. He'd only just started and he was as green as you are." Carter chuckled as he recalled something. "Seems he got the job through knocking up the Old Man's daughter. Obviously the Guv'nor thought the best way to get rid of an unwelcome suitor was to employ him."

"Very amusing," said Anthony.

"That's what I thought," said Carter. "Anyway, like I said, he lasted two whole years. Must have made close to a million dollars in that time."

"That should have made him very happy," said Anthony.

"I warned him a couple of times. 'Charlie,' I said, 'set yourself a target; so much money in the bank, then quit.' He agreed with me that it was a good idea. He obviously set his target too high. If he'd have settled for half a million dollars. he'd be living it up on the French Riviera right now. You might to do the same thing. Set yourself a target."

"I already have."

"Good man! Is it rude to ask how much?"

"Two thousand seven hundred dollars."

*   *   *

After they had finished their drinks, Carter took Anthony out to show him his consignment. At one end of the third warehouse had been stacked five hundred crates, each holding twenty rifles, and two hundred smaller crates each holding five thousand rounds of ammunition.

"That's your lot," said Carter, pointing them out.

"What am I supposed to do with them?"

"We load them on to the trucks and they're driven to the docks where they're transferred to the ship. Then you're on your own."

"What ship?"

"The *Maria*. She docks at oh four hundred tomorrow. You should be away on the evening tide."

"I go on the ship, too?"

"Naturally."

Anthony loathed ships. He was frightened of the sea and never failed to get sick. "I thought I might fly over and meet the boat the other end." he said.

Carter laughed. "Very droll," he said. "Now come on and I'll show you how to demonstrate the shooter."

He had an African break open one of the crates and extract a rifle. There was grease in the barrel and over all the working parts. Working efficiently, Carter stripped the rifle down, cleaned it thoroughly and reassembled it. Anthony watched carefully at first, but halfway through the operation his stomach started to rumble once more, and his headache to come back. So he lost interest and when finally Carter asked him something, his mind was a thousand miles away.

"Mmm? I'm sorry. What did you say?"

"Demonstration time," said Carter. "You're going to have to show the customer how to use it."

"Doesn't everyone know how to use a rifle?"

"Do you?"

"Not absolutely," said Anthony. "I mean, I know how to shoot it."

"You've got to load it first."

"Quite."

Carter showed him how to load it, where the safety catch was located, the adjustable rear sight, the hollow in the butt where the pull through was kept, the bolt action, the magazine capacity, the loading from clips. And finally he showed him how to fire it. They moved out into the compound once more and half a dozen old cans were set up on the perimeter fence two hundred yards away. Carter hit four of them with four shots; then he handed the rifle to Anthony, who fired three magazines and didn't hit anything at all.

"Never mind," said Carter. "You know how it should be done, even if you can't do it yourself."

Anthony handed the rifle back to Carter who turned it over to one of the Africans. The African started to grease the rifle again, preparatory to repacking it in its crate.

"Want to make a spot check?" enquired Carter.

"Of what?"

"You've only got my word for it that each of those crates holds twenty rifles."

"Your word is good enough for me."

"Start loading then?"

"Start loading."

Carter slapped him on the back. "Good man!" he said. Then he turned towards the Africans and gabbled something in the impossible local tongue. Immediately the Africans started to load the crates. Trucks were started up and driven to the doors of the warehouse where the crates were passed up and stacked into their rear. Within five minutes of giving the order, the first truck was already lumbering out of the compound. Apparently satisfied with the way things were going, Carter offered to drive Anthony back into town.

"Good idea to get to bed early tonight," he said. "We start loading the ship at four-thirty tomorrow morning."

Anthony nodded towards the group of Africans who were now loading the third truck. "They seem very efficient. They won't need me."

Carter shook his head. "These boys are good because they work for me. That lot down at the docks are a bunch of layabouts. Unless you stay with them every single minute they'll take all week to load the boat. You be there at four-thirty, old man. Take my word for it."

There didn't seem much else he could do, so Anthony agreed. "Will you be coming?" he asked.

"I'll be there at the start; show you the manifests; introduce you to the Captain. Then I'll have to leave you. Got to go up country tomorrow." He noticed that Anthony wasn't looking as happy as he might have been. "No problems, are there, old man?"

Anthony thought about the dead Charlie, his stomach, his headache, his prickly heat, his forthcoming boat trip with the inevitable seasickness. He thought about the customer waiting for him at the other end, and what he had learned about customer-dealer relations. He thought about all that and the fact that he was three thousand miles from home and Shirleen and about to become even farther.

"No problems," he said to Carter.

*   *   *

102

He arranged for the hotel to call him at four a.m. Carter was due to pick him up at four-fifteen and as he had no intention of washing or shaving, he considered that fifteen minutes would be all the time he would need to get ready. Unfortunately the night porter couldn't tell the time, and Anthony found himself being shaken at three-fifteen. He groped his way up out of sleep to see the porter grinning down at him.

"Is wake-up time," said the porter.

By the time Anthony realised that it wasn't wake-up time, he was too wide awake to want to go back to sleep again. So, with an hour to kill, he decided to take a bath after all. Then he discovered that there was no water coming from the taps in the bathroom. Enquiry of the porter elicited the fact that there never was any water between the hours of ten at night and six in the morning. This condition it seemed didn't only apply to the hotel, but to the whole of Manville. And with no water, there was no coffee or tea, and nothing to put in the whisky he poured himself except another whisky. Miraculously his stomach seemed to have settled down and his headache to have disappeared. No doubt his prickly heat would start acting up once the sun came up, but at this hour in the morning it was far too cold.

It was so cold, in fact, that he found his teeth chattering as he waited outside the hotel for Carter to arrive. That's all I need now, he thought, a good solid head cold to accompany my seasickness. He was on the point of asking the porter to fetch him a rug, when he heard the sound of an approaching jeep. A moment later he saw the headlamps at the end of the street, and he walked down from the hotel entrance to meet it.

Carter was wrapped in a large military great-coat, woollen

muffler, and thick gloves. He looked surprised to see Anthony without a coat. "Aren't you cold?" he asked, as Anthony climbed in.

"Freezing."

"Why aren't you wearing a coat?"

"I didn't think anyone wore an overcoat in Africa."

"They should have told you," said Carter. "Here, take a pull of this." He passed him a flask, and Anthony took a long swallow of brandy. It rested easily on top of the scotch he had already drunk and, although most of him was perishing cold, his stomach radiated a solid warmth.

"All the stuff is down at the docks," said Carter, as Anthony handed the flask back to him. "Soon as we arrive, they can start loading."

"Is my cabin ready?" asked Anthony.

"I suppose so," said Carter. "But you don't sail until this evening."

"That doesn't mean I'm not going to use it."

Carter looked a little worried. "Don't forget what I told you, old man. You've got to watch these dockside labourers. Keep on at them all the time."

"Don't worry," said Anthony. "Just find me the largest, meanest looking man on the dock."

"What for?"

"I shall give him fifty pounds when we start loading. For every hour we are loading I shall take five pounds back."

Carter grinned at him. "You're learning, old man."

*   *   *

The ss *Maria* weighed fifteen thousand tons, including the rust. She was built in Scotland in 1927, was sunk twice during World War Two, dredged up each time and put back to work. She had been sent to the breakers' yards on three separate occasions, but each time someone had stepped in with an offer about ten percent higher than her scrap value, so she hadn't been allowed to die. She was like a very, very old lady who was being kept alive against all odds by greedy relatives who saw more value in her working than in allowing her to give up the long overdue ghost.

As soon as they arrived at the dockside, Carter took Anthony on board to meet the Master. Captain McGraw was a Scotsman. He had been with the *Maria* for ten years and had loathed every minute of it. He hated every rivet, every plate, every patch of rust, every porthole, deck plank and rail on the ship. His hatred was almost pathological and he would spend half his waking hours cursing everything he could see. His hatred naturally overflowed on to everything connected with the ship, the crew, the cargo, and anyone unfortunate enough to be sailing as passenger. They found him on the bridge.

"This is Mr. Bridges, Captain. He'll be sailing with you," said Carter.

McGraw glared at Anthony from beneath a pair of the bushiest eyebrows he had ever seen. "Just keep your hands off my crew," he said by way of greeting.

"I beg your pardon?" said Anthony.

"I'll not tolerate any of your filthy homosexual habits on board my ship."

"I'm not a homosexual," said Anthony.

"The first time I catch you upping the cabin boy, I'll throw you over the side."

"I have no intention of upping anybody," said Anthony.

"Just let me catch you at it, that's all," said McGraw. "Now I'm off to get my head down. I'll thank you not to

make any clatter while you're loading. Good day to you."
He stalked off the bridge, kicking the compass housing in passing.

Next Carter introduced him to the First Mate. "Mr. Doyle, this is Mr. Bridges." Doyle was small, Irish, drunk and filthy. Anthony held out his hand and Doyle made to take it; he missed it by a good four inches and only managed to stay upright by hanging on to the wheel.

"Glad to have you aboard Mr ... Mr ..."

"Bridges," said Anthony, helpfully.

"Aye," said Doyle. Then his eyes focused vaguely and he seemed to see Anthony for the first time. He smiled, exposing a set of badly fitting false teeth. "You'll be sailing with us?"

"That's right."

"That's nice," said Doyle and, as Anthony stepped past him, following Carter off the bridge, he felt Doyle pat his backside tenderly.

Anthony caught up with Carter quickly. "He made a pass at me," he said, horror-struck.

"He always does," said Carter. "Just tell him you'll report him to the Captain. He's scared stiff of McGraw, ever since the Old Man threw him overboard in the Indian Ocean."

"Are you sure I can't fly over and meet the ship the other end?" asked Anthony.

"Positive," said Carter. "Come on, let's get the loading under way."

They walked back down to the dock. The crates that had been arriving all through the previous day were stacked high on the wharf. Five of Carter's Africans were still with them as guards and now, as it started to get light, the dockworkers were beginning to arrive. These men were town dwellers, distinguished as such by the fact that they were wearing shorts,

106

while their country brethren from Hengun only ran to breech clouts.

"Let's find your foreman," said Carter. "After that you can take it easy."

"What about him?" suggested Anthony, pointing to a massive Negro who was walking slowly towards them, scratching himself vigorously. Carter called out something and the Negro looked towards them. Realising that Carter was talking to him, he shambled over. Carter said something to him and he shook his head. Carter tried again, and again he shook his head, this time more positively. Carter tried once more, and this time he got an affirmative reaction. Carter turned to Anthony.

"How's your French?"

"Schoolboy."

'Should do," said Carter. "He speaks French."

Anthony looked at the Negro again. He really was enormous, well over six foot three, and half as wide as he was tall. He had small, mean looking eyes and was totally hairless.

"Do you think he'll do?" he asked Carter.

"You won't find anyone larger, that's for sure."

Anthony made up his mind. "All right. Tell him the arrangement."

"Which is?"

"I've got fifty pounds. One hour from now I shall deduct five pounds from it, and another five every hour until the ship is loaded. As soon as everything is stowed away, he is to report to me and I'll give him whatever's left. That way, if he loads the boat in four hours he'll get thirty pounds." He stood back and watched while Carter started to put the deal across. It took fifteen minutes. At first the Negro thought that he

107

was the one who was going to have to come across with the fifty pounds and he nearly hit Carter. Then Carter started again and gradually got through to him. Finally, with a huge grin, the Negro turned to Anthony, nodding his bullet-shaped head vigorously.

"*Oui, oui,*" he said. "*D'accord.*"

Anthony managed a small smile. "*Bon,*" he said. "*Très bon.*"

The Negro nodded his head some more. "*Oui, Très bon Très, très bon.*" Then, when Anthony didn't say anything else, the Negro's smile started to crack around the edges. "*Où est l'argent?*" he asked.

"What did he say?" Anthony asked Carter.

"He wants to see the money."

Anthony pulled out his wallet and extracted ten five pound notes. He held them up, showing them to the Negro, who beamed again. "*Bon. Très bon,*" he said, then turned and started bellowing at the other dock workers who were still straggling up. One of them gave him a slight argument, and wound up flat on his back with a bloody nose and minus three teeth. After that everything went like clockwork. Carter introduced Anthony to the Third Officer of the *Maria* who was to supervise the stowing of the cargo. He was a large, mild mannered Sikh who obviously knew his job and who hoped that by doing it well and minding his own business, he would be able to transfer away from the *Maria* at the earliest possible date. By five-fifteen the first load was already being swung aboard and Carter decided that he could leave. He handed Anthony a large, sealed envelope.

"Here are your delivery instructions, old man. As soon as you leave the harbour bar, old man McGraw will come to you for his sailing orders. They're all here. Just tell him

108

where you want to go and what time you want to get there. He'll do the rest."

"Providing I don't up the cabin boy," said Anthony, who was feeling quite pleased with himself at the way he had handled the loading situation.

Carter grinned. "You haven't seen the cabin boy." He stuck out his hand. "See you next time through."

"I doubt it," said Anthony.

Carter looked at him shrewdly for a moment. "You'll be back."

"What makes you say that?"

"You'll get home from this venture with a few thousand dollars in the bank. You'll decide that a few thousand dollars isn't enough."

"Enough for what?"

"For anything."

"It is when you've never had a few thousand dollars."

"Want to make a bet?"

Anthony thought about it for a moment, then he shook his head. "No bet," he said. "If I win, I won't be around to collect."

Carter grinned again and the two of them walked over to where Carter had parked the jeep. He shouted across to his five Africans, who ran over and climbed into the back, chattering among themselves. Carter got into the driving seat and started the engine.

"Don't forget," he said, just before he drove off. "Never turn your back on a satisfied customer."

5

ANTHONY'S CABIN WASN'T AS BAD AS HE HAD supposed. Apart from the bunk, which was wide and looked very comfortable, there was a small desk, a couple of easy chairs and a large closet. A tiny bathroom led off the cabin and because it was situated on the main deck, there were windows instead of portholes. Having seen Carter off, Anthony spent fifteen minutes at the dockside watching the loading; then realising there was nothing for him to do, he located his cabin, unpacked, and with a certain amount of trepidation rang the bell fixed above his bunk. It was answered by a man whom Anthony later learned was the cabin boy; he was also the steward and the officers' cook. Well over sixty years old,

110

oriental and very polite, he came into the cabin bowing and didn't straighten up fully until he had backed his way out again.

"Yes, sir. I speak English. My name is Wong," he said in answer to Anthony's enquiry.

"Could I have some breakfast, please?" asked Anthony.

"What sort breakfast you having?"

"What sort have you got?"

"Bacon, eggs, steak, ham, chicken, porridge, whisky, tea, coffee, pancakes, gin, potato chips, tripe, onions, livers, kidney pie, vodka, pork chops."

Anthony's stomach gave a little lurch. "Just some tea and toast, please," he said.

"Tea, toast . . . Yes, sir," said Wong, as he bobbed his way backwards out of the cabin.

Anthony waited until he had finished his breakfast before opening the envelope that Carter had handed him. The first thing he read was a letter clipped to the top of a pile of other papers. There was no heading to the letter; it just started right off.

The consignment (see inventory, attachment No. 1) is to be delivered to Miguel Canstartis (see biographical details, attachment No. 2) at Canstartisville, the capital city of Santhoma (see geographical and political details, attachment No. 3). The Master of the vessel is to be given the enclosed sailing instructions (attachment No. 4). Having made contact with Miguel Canstartis (see instructions and identification codes, attachment No. 5) you will forward a cable addressed to HENGUN LONDON *with the one word "Ready". On no acount will you deliver the consignment to Canstartis until you receive a reply by cable with the one word "Go". This will*

111

confirm that payment has been made in Switzerland. Upon receipt of this cable you are at liberty to turn the consignment over to Canstartis. You will then return to London by any means available. These instructions must be rigidly adhered to.

There was no signature. Anthony read it through again; then he turned to the attachments. The first was a detailed inventory of the consignment, virtually a copy of the list that Carter had handed him earlier the previous day.

10,000 short magazine Lee Enfield rifles, Mark IV, packed in 500 cases of twenty rifles per case.
1,000,000 rounds of ammunition for same, packed in 200 cases of 5,000 rounds per case.

Each crate was numbered and the inventory ran to four closely typed foolscap pages. Attachment number two was headed MIGUEL CANSTARTIS, and Anthony put it aside to read later. He wanted to know where he was going before he bothered with whom he was supposed to meet when he got There. The next attachment was headed SANTHOMA, and was subdivided into two sections, "Geographical" and "Political". Anthony started in to read the first section.

Santhoma is a country located on the West coast of the South American continent. It runs for a total of four hundred and eighty miles from North to South, and attains a maximum East to West width of fifty miles. It is bordered on the West by the Pacific Ocean, and on the North, East and South by a high range of mountains which effectively cut it off from the remainder of the South American continent. The population figure at the last census (1922) was put at four million three

112

hundred thousand. It may be assumed, however, that since that time, due to the climate, which is hot, and the fact that ninety-eight per cent of the population are ardent Catholics, the population will have increased by not less than thirty-five per cent. This increase takes into account the very high infant mortality rate and the generally low life expectancy. (In 1934 a leading American insurance company had actuarial figures drawn up prior to opening a branch in Santhoma. Life expectancy was calculated at forty-two years. The insurance company did not subsequently follow up its plans to open up a branch.) The country is virtually self supporting, due mainly to the fact that it exports nothing, and is consequently unable to earn the foreign currency necessary to pay for imports. The climate can be described loosely as tropical, with a rainy season lasting from early September through to the following May. During the dry season, the average daily temperature is ninety-eight degrees Fahrenheit. The capital city is situated on the coast, about midway between the North and South borders. It is at present named Canstartisville (see attachment No. 2, Miguel Canstartis). Before this it has been named Tuloville, Fuentesville, Quintannaville, Maessoville and others; the name of the capital depending on who holds political power at the time. The people of Santhoma are a hardy race, intensely political, uncommunicative to foreigners, volatile, and generally considered difficult to deal with. The language spoken is a mixture of Spanish and Portugese with a heavy influence of pure South American Indian dialect which Westerners usually find difficult to master. Agriculture is maintained at a level sufficient to feed the populace, although there have been major famines in the years 1958, 1949, 1942, 1933 and 1921.

113

Industry is entirely local and State owned and run. There is no tourist industry.

That doesn't surprise me, thought Anthony, putting the top page aside and starting on the second. This was headed "Political".

Politics have long been the major preoccupation of the people of Santhoma. It is useless to try to define the major political influences by ordinary standards, as the variations from one party to another – and among individuals in the same party – are too great for any person not born and bred in Santhoma to comprehend. Briefly, however, there are two main parties at any one time; the party that is in power, and the party that isn't. As soon as the party that is not in power overthrows the party that is, then another party springs up to take its place as the party that isn't in power.

Anthony read this last bit through twice more before continuing . . .

The basic constitution of the country, drawn up in 1905, provides for general elections on the democratic principle of one man, one vote. However, due to the constant shifting in power, invariably brought about by revolutionary process, no one government has been in office long enough to hold such an election. The current President is Miguel Canstartis (see attachment No. 2). He has held that position for eighteen months. There is no evidence that either of the two major power blocs, the Americans or the Russians, have any interest or influence in the political structure of this country, It is believed that Red China at one time tried to exert some influence in Santhoma, but due to a wide-spread Santhomese superstition that Orientals are directly descended from the

Devil, they are not allowed to land in the country or, if they do, they are invariably burned at the stake on public holidays. To summarise, the politics of Santhoma are pure Fascist with a strong leaning to the Left or, depending who is in power at that moment, to the Right.

Now I know where I'm going, thought Anthony, let's see whom I'm going to meet. He turned back to Attachment No. 2. It was headed MIGUEL CANSTARTIS.

The early life of Canstartis is shrouded in uncertainty. It is likely, however, that he was born in Santhoma, but he probably left that country early in his childhood and received his education elsewhere. He speaks fluent English and French, an accomplishment he could not have attained under the Santhomese educational system. He was first heard of during the Revolution of 1965 (the Spring Revolution; not to be confused with Autumn one of the same year). As a result of this revolution, Sergio Quintanna became the country's new President, and Canstartis was appointed his Chief Minister, no doubt as reward for the support he gave to Quintanna during and before the uprising. In the Autumn Revolution of the same year, Canstartis managed to avoid capture by the forces of Juan Tulo, when Tulo came to power. (Quintanna was apprehended crossing the border with two million dollars worth of gold which he had taken from the Treasury. He was subsequently beheaded in the main square of the capital, then Tuloville, on all Saints Day 1966.) It is likely that Canstartis took to the hills at this time and joined forces with Gustavo Fuentes, because when Fuentes mounted his revolution in 1968, Canstartis was already a member of his staff. It was Canstartis who arranged through intermediaries to purchase 5,000 rifles from Hengun Inc. to arm the Revolution-

115

aries. He was created Chief Minister once more, a position he held under Fuentes until 1969, when he arranged the murder of the President and subsequently took the title himself. He held power until late that year, when an ill-conceived and badly organised uprising under the leadership of Manuel Pescardo, temporarily left the country without an effective government. Eventually Pescardo was forced to flee without ever having formed a Government or declaring himself President; this was brought about when Canstartis mounted a successful coup, this time with himself at the head. In this he was assisted by the army, due to the fact that he was able to buy their loyalty with money that he had looted from the treasury during his last tenure in office. He thus became President for the second time (1970) and has held that office ever since. There have been three subsequent attempts to depose him, each one unsuccessful. Miguel Canstartis is approximately forty-five years old; he is physically a strong man, cruel and completely despotic. When dealing with him it is strongly advised that he never be trusted. He is married and has three children by his wife. The family live quietly in a heavily guarded villa twenty kilometres outside the city of Canstartisville.

*　　*　　*

Anthony put the notes aside and decided that he would go on deck and check how the loading was progressing. Then he changed his mind. His newly created foreman had been told to report to him as soon as everything was on board, and he didn't feel there was anything he could do that the giant African couldn't do better. He rang for Wong again and told him to bring him a cup of tea at midday. Then he got undressed and went to bed. Two hours later he was rudely awakened. He groped up out of sleep to see his African foreman grinning down at him and at the same time shaking him vigorously by the shoulder.

"*Il est fait*," the Negro was saying. "*Il est fait.*"

Anthony took a couple of moments to realise that the man was talking French and a couple more to make out what he was saying. Then he sat up in bed and looked at his watch. It was ten o'clock exactly. As though to confirm the time the Negro stuck out one huge hand, palm upwards.

"*Vingt cinq*," he said. "*Vingt cinq.*"

"*Un moment*," said Anthony. "*Excusez moi.*" The African stood back while Anthony climbed out of bed.

"*Vingt cinq*," he kept muttering while Anthony pulled an a shirt and some trousers. "*Cinq heures à dix heures. Vingt cinq.*" He followed Anthony up on to the deck, still muttering, and he didn't stop until Anthony had checked that everything was indeed aboard and started to pay him. He stuffed the twenty-five pounds in the pocket of his shorts and then held out his hand again.

"*Plus*," he said.

"*Pourquoi plus?*" asked Anthony.

"*Plus*," repeated the Negro. Anthony held up his wrist watch, showing him the time; then he pantomimed five hours back. "*Plus*," said the African, unimpressed. Anthony, who always liked to take the line of least resistance, gave him his *plus*. He peeled off another fiver and, when the African remained with his hand stuck out, two more. At last the man seemed satisfied. He smiled hugely, slapped Anthony on the back, and marched off down the gangplank, waving his extra money over his head and shouting at his fellow dock workers. They raised a little cheer for him and the whole lot of them started trooping away as though off to a party.

117

The Third Officer came up beside Anthony and stood leaning on the rail, watching them. "They will all be drunk for a week now," he said. "You shouldn't have given him so much."

"Did you see how large he was?" said Anthony, who was feeling quite pleased with himself.

The Third Officer shrugged. "You shouldn't have given him so much." Then he pulled himself together. "Everything is stowed away. Do you wish to check it?"

Perhaps I should, thought Anthony, but as he had no idea what he would do if he found anything missing, he declined the offer. He thanked the Third Officer and returned to his cabin. There he went to bed again to be woken at midday by Wong with a large cup of tea in his hand.

"Captain him want to see you soon," said Wong.

"Ask him to come down," said Anthony.

"Captain him never go no place 'cept bridge and cabin."

"Never?"

Wong shook his head. "Never. He don't go no place now for five years. He don't go ashore, he don't go down hold, he don't go engine room or crew quarters. He don't go no place 'cept bridge and cabin."

*   *   *

Anthony pushed Wong out of his cabin and got dressed. He collected the sailing orders from his desk and went to find the Captain. He wasn't on the bridge, but Doyle was.

"Where can I find the Captain, please?" asked Anthony.

"In his cabin."

"Where's that?"

"Shouldn't disturb him now if I was you," said Doyle. "Why not come down to my cabin instead? We'll have a drink."

118

"No, thank you."

"Some other time then. It's going to be a long voyage."

"Indeed it is," said Anthony. "Now please will you tell me where the Captain's cabin is?"

Doyle pointed along a companionway that led from the back of the bridge. "End door. Can't miss it."

Anthony thanked him and moved off down the companionway. The door at the end was closed. There was a wooden plaque nailed to it with the words MON REPOS carved into it. He knocked and a moment later he heard McGraw tell him to come in. The cabin consisted of two inter-connecting rooms. The far room was the bedroom, and Anthony could see through the half open door what looked like the end of an old brass bedstead, the bed itself covered with a patchwork quilt. The near room, the one he was standing in, was obviously the living room. It had been made to look as unnautical as possible; all ship-type furniture and fittings had been stripped out and replaced with the sort of furniture that would be found in a Victorian parlour or a present-day junk shop. There were two velvet buttoned armchairs with grubby antimacassars slung over the backs; there was an upright piano with brass candelabra sprouting from each side; there were small, busy little tables and padded footstools; there was wax fruit under glass; and there were framed daguerreotypes hanging on the walls. McGraw himself was sitting in one of the armchairs, his feet resting on a footstool. He was wearing an old flannel dressing-gown, carpet slippers, and his Master's peaked cap. There was an open book on his knee that Anthony just knew had to be by Charles Dickens.

"Aye," he said, as Anthony came in. "What do you want?"

"You wanted to see me."

"Oh, aye," said McGraw, remembering. Then he looked suspicious suddenly. "You haven't been messing around with the crew have you?" Anthony assured him he hadn't, and McGraw growled at him. "See that you don't! Can't abide homosexuals on my ship. Throw 'em overboard."

"I'm not a homosexual," said Anthony. "And here are your sailing orders."

McGraw took them, still looking at Anthony suspiciously. "You look like one," he said.

"Well I'm not."

"Mmm," said the Captain, unconvinced. Then he changed the subject. "Cargo aboard?" Anthony nodded. "Battened down?"

"I assume so."

"We can get out of this heathen hell-hole, then?"

"As far as I am concerned, we can," said Anthony politely.

McGraw then seemed to dismiss him from his mind as he started to tear open the sailing orders. Assuming he wasn't wanted any more, Anthony turned and started out of the cabin. McGraw delivered a parting shot just before he left. "You talk like one too," he said.

*　　　*　　　*

Anchor was weighed at three-thirty p.m. There were no tugs at Lamboola and McGraw had to ease the *Maria* out on her own. This he did with a series of manoeuvres that had her clouting the sides of the dock vigorously each time he reversed the engines to get a little more room to see his way out to clear water. Anthony, who was leaning on the forerail, was reminded of a man whose car has been parked too close to those in front and behind him and who proceeds to bash his way out. But finally McGraw judged that the bow was

120

pointing in the right direction. He rang down for "Full ahead" and the *Maria* started to lurch her way out to sea.

The moment they cleared the harbour bar, sideswiping it once on the way out, Anthony started to feel sick. He debated for a moment whether he was better off up on deck or whether he should retreat to the sanctuary of his cabin; then his mind was made up for him as he heard his name called. He looked up to see McGraw leaning over the bridge rail, looking down at him.

"Did you no hear me?" McGraw yelled.

"I heard you, Captain. What do you want?"

"I want to talk. Get yourself up here."

Anthony clambered up to the bridge, feeling worse by the second. Apart from the helmsman, a disgruntled looking lascar, McGraw was alone on the bridge.

"I take it you know where we're heading?" he said as soon as Anthony appeared.

"Santhoma."

"Aye. Santhoma. That Godforsaken, idolatrous, heathen hell-hole."

"I thought the population were Catholic."

"Aye. That's what I said," said McGraw. "Now which way would you be wanting to go?"

"Is there a choice?" asked Anthony.

"Of course there is, man. We can go round the Cape or we can use the Canal."

"Which is the quickest?"

"There's no difference, or I'd not be asking you."

"I really don't mind then," said Anthony, whose only desire was to get off the bridge before he was sick.

"Good," said McGraw. "We'll go round the Cape." He turned to the helmsman. "Left a wee bit," he said. The lascar

121

repeated the order with exactly the same intonation. "Left a wee bit," he said, turning the wheel to port.

McGraw turned back to Anthony. "Ye'll be taking your daily lunch with me in my cabin," he said. "Dinner you'll be having in the saloon with the other officers." It was an order, not a request, and Anthony nodded mutely. "Now I'll thank you to clear off my bridge."

Gratefully Anthony retreated. As he clambered down the steps to the deck, he heard McGraw shouting at the helmsman. "I said left a *wee* bit. Do you no understand a simple nautical term when you hear it?" This was followed by the sound of a blow, but Anthony was past caring. He just managed to make the rail before throwing up into a sea that was as calm and as flat as a millpond.

*　　*　　*

The first part of the voyage passed uneventfully, if one discounted the visitor that Anthony received on the second evening out. He was sick for the first two days, and remained in his cabin, slowly dying. Wong would appear from time to time in an effort to tempt him into eating something. He finally gave up trying after Anthony threw a shoe at his head at the same time as he was throwing up the contents of his empty stomach. After that, Anthony was left alone until the evening of the second day.

He was lying on his bunk, bracing himself against the non-existent roll of the ship, when there was a light tap on his door. Thinking it was Wong coming to tempt him with more food, he managed to squeeze a remarkable amount of venom into his voice and shouted, "Fuck off!" A moment later, the door opened tentatively and a woman came into his cabin.

122

She was a veritable harridan, raddled beyond belief; she had violently orange hair, a slash of bright red lipstick, rouged cheeks and an expression that was supposed to be roguish, but to Anthony looked repulsively predatory. She was wearing a vivid green dress made of cheap silk, thick stockings, and impossibly high heels which turned sideways with each step she took, threatening to break the wearer's ankles. In her right hand she carried a beaded purse and in her left a bottle of rum. For one desperate moment Anthony thought he was hallucinating; then she spoke.

"I just popped in to see how you were, ducky," said Doyle.

"Oh my God!" said Anthony.

"Feeling a bit peaky, are we? I've brought along some medicine. We'll have a nice quiet drink, you and me. Soon have you up." Doyle giggled. "If you'll pardon the expression."

Anthony summoned his remaining strength. "Mister Doyle," he said, laying particular emphasis on the "Mister". "If you don't get out of here, I will throw you overboard myself. After that I will tell the Captain, who will no doubt do the same."

Doyle's face crumpled beneath its make-up. "Oh dear," he said. He looked at Anthony for a moment, then without another word, turned and tottered out. He closed the door behind him, but a second later he shoved it open again, sticking his head into say, "Please don't tell the Captain."

"I won't tell him if you promise to behave yourself for the rest of the voyage."

Doyle agreed readily, and the affair was never mentioned again.

*　　*　　*

123

Later that night the weather started to freshen and as it deteriorated, so Anthony began to feel better. He ordered an enormous breakfast from Wong on the third day and put it all away, even being tempted to ask for seconds. Then he dressed and went up on deck. The sea was green where it had been blue, and he decided he liked it better that way. The *Maria* was making heavy weather of her progress although the sea was only mildly rough. Anthony decided that if genuine rough weather appeared, the *Maria* would go straight to the bottom upside down and, strange to relate, he didn't seem to mind one little bit. It was such a relief not to feel sea sick any longer that he would have been perfectly content if he had been told he only had another three months to live. His euphoria was somewhat shattered when McGraw shouted down to him from the bridge. "Don't forget you'll be taking your lunch in my cabin. One o'clock sharp."

Anthony waved his acknowledgement and then decided to explore the ship. He had been on board for three days already and, apart from his cabin, the bridge, and a quick visit to the cargo hold before they sailed, he had seen nothing. Half an hour later he realised that there was nothing to see; the *Maria* was scruffy, barely functional and, as far as Anthony could make out, with his limited knowledge of such things, held together by the rust that seemed to have eaten away a good thirty per cent of her iron work. The decks were oily, the hand rails slippery, the superstructure grubby. The crew members he had seen during his short tour were all lascars and an extremely disgruntled looking lot. His "good mornings" were answered by scowls, and every attempt he made to strike up a conversation was met by stony silence.

*　　*　　*

Lunch turned out to be as uncomfortable as Anthony had feared. When he reported to Mon Repos at exactly one o'clock, McGraw was waiting for him. The Captain had removed his uniform jacket, exposing a pair of bright red, frayed braces; he had changed into his carpet slippers again, but he still wore his uniform cap.

"Come in! Come in!" he said to Anthony, who was hesitating just inside the door. "Have a glass of sherry."

Anthony had his glass of sherry, sickly sweet, and then sat down to lunch served by Wong. The food was almost uneatable; obviously McGraw had his meals specially prepared, thought Anthony, because no ship's crew was going to stand for what he and the Captain were eating.

"Curried haggis," said McGraw without preamble.

"Delicious," said Anthony.

"We've got porridge for afters."

"That will be nice."

"Always believe in eating well. Curried haggis and porridge every day."

Anthony looked up. "Every day?"

"Been having it for the past five years now. A couple of weeks lunching with me, laddy, and you'll be a real man."

"I'm not a homosexual," said Anthony, his self-defensive reflexes springing to attention.

"Never said you were," said McGraw. Then he looked at Anthony suspiciously. "But as long as you've brought it up, do you know what I do to homosexuals I find on board my ship?"

"You throw them overboard."

"How did you know that?"

"You told me. Twice."

"Probably did. Tell everyone who sets foot on board. So

watch it, young fellow." After that McGraw launched himself into a tirade of condemnation embracing Jews, Catholics, Negroes, Communists, Englishmen and, of course, homosexuals.

"Never go ashore these days," he said. "Don't like what's going on there. Haven't been ashore now for five years."

"You stay on the ship all the time?"

"Why not? Happy ship. I always run a happy ship."

At this moment the door opened and Doyle came in. "Trouble, Captain," he said, after batting his eyelids once at Anthony.

"What sort of trouble, Mister?"

"The crew have mutinied."

Anthony felt a chill of fear, but McGraw didn't seem unduly concerned. He pulled a key from his trouser pocket and getting up from the table he walked over to an intricately carved Victorian bureau, set against one of the walls. He unlocked it, pulled open a drawer, and started to take out revolvers. He stuffed one into the waistband of his trousers, handed one to Doyle and after a moment's hesitation passed one to Anthony. "Where are the other officers?" he asked Doyle.

"The Chief is down in the engine room. He just called up to say he's locked himself in a chain-locker. Ram Singh is on the bridge."

"Where's Sparks?"

"You threw him overboard last trip. We didn't manage to pick up a replacement in Lamboola."

"Oh aye," said McGraw. "I remember now." He turned to Anthony. "Stay close to me, young fellow," he said. Then he turned and headed for the door.

Having had a good look at the crew that morning,

126

Anthony wasn't at all sure that he was on the right side; he followed the Captain, wondering what the penalty would be for a passenger who joined the mutineers. But the Captain and Doyle looked reasonably confident in their ability to handle the situation, neither of them appearing particularly worried; and after all, thought Anthony, we're the ones who are armed.

"They've got guns," said Singh as they walked on to the bridge.

"Where the hell did they get those?" asked McGraw.

"They broke into the cargo hold."

The three officers looked at Anthony accusingly. "What have you got down there?" asked McGraw.

"Rifles."

"Ammunition?"

"A million rounds."

McGraw made an expression of disgust. "We may be having a wee bit of a problem then."

Seeing that he was obviously going to be shouldered with some of the blame, Anthony decided he'd better find out what was going on. "Excuse me," he said, interrupting the huddle the officers had gone into. They turned towards him. "What exactly are they mutinying for?"

"Who the hell knows," growled McGraw. "Last time it was the food."

"It's happened before?"

"Aye, many times."

"What did you do?"

"Shot a couple of them."

"Couldn't you have improved the food?"

"There was nothing wrong with the food. Same as I ate meself."

127

Anthony started to feel even more sympathy for the mutineers, but he seemed committed now, and there wasn't much he could do about it. Looking out from the bridge, he couldn't see a soul on the foredeck. He turned to the officers again; they had finished their huddle; McGraw was leaning against the compass housing, idly spinning the chamber of his revolver; Doyle was seated on a stool, his back up against the rear of the bridge housing, picking his nose; Ram Singh was scratching his beard ruminatively. There was nobody at the wheel and Anthony realised for the first time that the engines had stopped. Except for the noise of the sea slapping against the *Maria's* hull, there wasn't a sound.

"Shouldn't we find out what they want?" said Anthony finally. "I know it's none of my business but . . ."

"It sure as hell is your business," said McGraw. "You're the one who brought those guns aboard."

"They've never had guns before," said Doyle to no-one in particular.

"Regardless of that," said Anthony. "I still think it would be a good idea to find out what they want."

"They sent a deputation last time," said Doyle.

"Will they this time?" asked Anthony.

"Doubt it," said Doyle. "The Captain shot them last time."

"Then surely it's up to us to go down and find out what their grievances are?"

"Not up to me," said McGraw. "I'm not mutinying."

Anthony looked towards Doyle, who shook his head. He turned to Ram Singh. "How about you, Mr. Singh?"

"Not me, sir. I am merely a lowly third officer."

There was another long silence, broken this time by McGraw. "They're your guns," he said.

128

"The Captain's right," said Doyle.

"Yes, sir, he certainly is," said Ram Singh. They were all looking at Anthony.

"I'm a passenger," said Anthony.

"You chartered the ship," said McGraw. "That makes you temporary owner. The owner outranks the Captain, doesn't he, Mister?"

"Oh yes, sir," said Doyle.

"Yes indeed," said Ram Singh.

"You mean you expect *me* to go down and talk to them?"

"Seems the only thing," said McGraw.

"I agree," said Doyle.

"I am agreeing also," said Singh.

"But what do I say to them?"

"Just ask them what they want, then tell them they can have it."

"Whatever it is?"

"Certainly. Once we get them up out of that hold, we don't have to give it to them."

"You'd go back on your word?"

"No," said McGraw. "But I'd go back on yours."

"I'm not going," said Anthony.

"Don't see that you've got any alternative," said McGraw

"Of course I have. If I say that I'm not going, that's an end to it. It's your mutiny; you handle it." McGraw stopped spinning the chamber of his revolver, and Doyle took his finger out of his nose. Neither of them said anything; Ram Singh was gazing out towards the distant horizon seeming to have lost interest in the entire conversation. Then the silence on the bridge was suddenly shattered by the buzz of the telephone. Doyle picked it up without getting off his stool.

"Bridge. Oh hello, Chief. What do you want?" There was

a short pause before he spoke again. "Yes, I'll tell him." He hung up and turned to McGraw. "The Chief says that if we don't get him out of the chain locker in ten minutes, he's going to join the mutiny."

"Why would he want to do that?" asked McGraw.

"He says because in ten minutes he will have suffocated to death."

"Can't have the Chief joining them," said McGraw. "He's a canny one. He'd get them organised." He turned to Anthony. "Off you go, young fellow."

"I told you. I'm not . . ." He stopped as he realised that McGraw's revolver was pointing straight at him. "Would you mind not pointing that gun at me," he said. "It makes me nervous."

The gun didn't waver. "The Chief said ten minutes. Better hurry along," said McGraw.

"Are you threatening me?" said Anthony, knowing the answer.

"Certainly not," said McGraw. "But I'd get a move on if I was you. Right, Mr. Doyle?"

"Right, Captain?"

"Oh yes," said Ram Singh, rejoining the company. "Most certainly."

So it boiled down to six of one, half a dozen of the other, thought Anthony. Either I stay up here and get shot, or I go downstairs and get shot. "Well, I'd better get moving," he said. "Which is the best way down to the hold?"

"I'll show you," said Doyle, jumping down from his stool. He walked with Anthony on to the exterior section of the bridge and pointed out the quickest route. Anthony handed his revolver to Doyle.

"Aren't you taking it with you?" asked Doyle.

130

"I don't think it would be a good idea."

"But they're armed."

"Exactly. There's about twenty-five of them and they have ten thousand rifles and a million rounds of ammunition between them.

Doyle looked at the revolver. "I see what you mean," he said. "Good luck." He scuttled back on to the bridge as Anthony started down to the main deck. Just before he reached the deck, McGraw leaned out of the bridge and shouted to him. "Don't mess around with any of the crew or I'll throw you overboard."

*   *   *

He found the crew in the main cargo hold. They had broken open a couple of the crates holding the rifles and one box of ammunition. There were about twenty of them, chattering away among themselves, clicking bolts, slamming magazines in and out, and generally enjoying themselves. Nobody took any notice of Anthony as he appeared in the hold and, after clearing his throat a couple of times, he was finally forced to shout to make his presence felt. "Excuse me," he said. Twenty heads swung towards him followed by the barrels of twenty rifles. There was a long silence during which time Anthony managed to clear his throat again. Finally one man detached himself from the others. He was large and mean looking; Anthony vaguely recalled seeing him in the engine room that morning arguing with a very fat, middle aged white man, who must have been the Chief.

"What do you want?" asked the man.

"I'm here on behalf of the Captain," said Anthony. "He wants to know what your grievances are." Most of the crew spoke no English and they immediately started asking what

131

Anthony had said. The mean looking one shouted them to silence, then turned back to Anthony.

"You tell Captain we want better food, more pay, shorter work, and better comfortable place to sleep."

"That sounds fair," said Anthony. "I'll tell him." He turned to go, but the man stopped him.

"Stay standing still," he said. He turned to another crew-member and said something to him. The second man shook his head vigorously.

"No," he said in English. "I not go."

"I am the leader of this mutiny. I say you go, you go."

"The Captain shoot me like he did last time."

"He no shoot you while we got prisoner."

That's it, thought Anthony, I'm a bloody hostage against a lunatic Captain who throws people overboard and shoots them as soon as look at them. But the logic of this argument got through to the second crewman and he finally agreed to go to see the Captain. He and the leader reverted to their native tongue for a few minutes, then the leader turned back to Anthony.

"My name Jamsir. What's yours?"

"Bridges. Anthony Bridges."

"All right, Mr. Bridges Anthony Bridges, you are staying here with us. The Captain does what we tell him, you O.K. He doesn't, we shoot you."

The man chosen as a negotiator selected a companion and the two of them left to present their case to McGraw. The remainder of the crew now grew bored with Anthony and started to play with their guns again; all except Jamsir, who told Anthony to sit down, and proceeded to mount guard over him. After about five minutes Anthony remembered something.

132

"Could we persuade the Chief to come out before he suffocates?" he asked.

Jamsir shrugged. "You tell him. He come out if he wants."

"Where is he?"

Accompanied by two others, Jamsir led Anthony through to the engine room and over to a small bulkhead door. He banged on the door with the butt of his rifle.

"Someone want to talk to you, Chief," he said.

A voice came from the other side of the door. "Go away, you stinking black heathen."

Jamsir grinned and indicated that Anthony should talk. "This is Anthony Bridges here," he said to the closed door. "I'm sure you'd be better off if you came out."

"Why?" came the voice.

"I understand you'll suffocate to death in about five minutes."

"Quite right," came the voice.

"Then why don't you come out?"

"Jamsir said he was going to throw me in the boiler."

Anthony looked at Jamsir who, still grinning, shook his head. "He won't do that," said Anthony.

"How do you know?"

"He just said so."

Something that sounded like a hollow laugh came from the other side of the door. Anthony tried again. "He's holding me as a hostage. He's prepared to do the same with you."

"Hostage against what?"

"The Captain granting their requests."

"I'll stay here," came the voice of the Chief.

"The Captain gave me his word that it would be all right."

"I'll still stay here."

133

Anthony began to lose his patience. "All right. Stay there and suffocate."

There was a short pause before the Chief spoke again. "Do you guarantee my safety?" he said through the door.

Why not? thought Anthony. "I guarantee it," he said.

There was another pause and then the sound of bolts being drawn back. A moment later the Chief stuck his head out. He was a short man, very fat, with small frightened eyes. "Who are you?" he said to Anthony.

"Anthony Bridges."

The Chief looked towards Jamsir, his eyes growing more frightened. "He's got a gun."

Jamsir grinned widely. "We all got guns." The Chief tried to back his way into the chain-locker once more, but Jamsir stepped forward, and leaning against the door, prevented it from closing. "Now I got two hostages," he said to no-one in particular. "This time the Captain do what we ask."

*   *   *

"Do they do this sort of thing often?" asked Anthony. He and the Chief were sitting to one side of the hold, guarded by a couple of the crew members.

"What sort of thing?" asked the Chief, who was still of the opinion that he would have been better off suffocating to death.

"Mutiny."

"Every third or fourth voyage."

"But aren't you supposed to be able to hang them or something? I mean, it's illegal, isn't it?"

"The Captain usually shoots a couple of them and lets the others off. He'd never have a crew if he didn't."

134

"What do the owners say about it?"

"The Captain's the owner. He bought the *Maria* five years ago when his Aunt Hetty died and left him some money."

"Crafty old sod," said Anthony, remembering how McGraw had tried to con him by telling him he was the temporary owner.

"He's certainly that," said the Chief. "He's also completely barmy."

"Why do you sail with him then?" asked Anthony.

The Chief looked a little embarrassed. "Lost my ticket a few years back," he said. "Can't be too choosy."

"Same with the other officers?"

The Chief nodded. Then he started to get red in the face beneath the engine oil. "Bloody old pirate," he said. "Doesn't pay us anything like a living wage; works the asses off us; has us carrying dodgy cargoes that no-one else will look at; and gets rich in the process. One day somebody is going to throw *him* overboard. I only hope I'm around when it happens." He glanced up at his armed guards and his expression became morose again. "Which ain't very likely in the circumstances."

"Cheer up," said Anthony. "He can't sail the *Maria* by himself. He'll just have to do what the crew are asking."

"Ha!" said the Chief, and relapsed once more into miserable silence. He hadn't said a further word when, ten minutes later, the two man delegation returned from their interview with the captain. Obviously negotiations hadn't gone according to plan, because one of them was supporting the other who was bleeding like a stuck pig screaming that the Captain had shot his balls off.

*   *   *

"Have you any last request?" Jamsir said to Anthony.

"Only that I'd rather you didn't shoot me."

"Hostages are for shooting," said Jamsir. "Afterwards we will throw your bullet riddled body up on to the deck for the Captain to see. If he still doesn't grant our requests we will do the same with the Chief."

"What happens after that?"

"Then we attack the bridge, shooting all of the officers. Do you want a blindfold?"

"No thank you. But there is one thing you can do for me."

"There, you *do* have a last request. What is it?"

"I would like you to lead the firing squad and shoot with them. You're obviously a good shot. I can tell that by the way you handle the rifle, and I want death to come quickly. I don't like to suffer."

Jamsir inclined his head at the compliment. "I shall be honoured," he said. "Now shall we get it over with?"

Anthony got to his feet. The Chief stuck out his hand. "Nice to have met you," he said.

"Likewise," said Anthony.

He was led across to the far side of the hold where a space had been cleared of cargo. There he was stood against the hull. Jamsir quickly detailed four men who, with himself, would comprise the firing squad. They lined up abreast at the opposite side of the hold.

"Ready," said Jamsir. "Aim!" The five rifles came up into line, all aimed more or less at Anthony's head.

"One moment, please," said Anthony. The rifles were all lowered at a command from Jamsir.

"What now?" he asked.

"Are you sure I can't talk you out of this?"

"I am sure."

"You're making a big mistake."

"I don't think so."

"Well, don't say I didn't warn you," said Anthony, drawing himself up straight, sticking out his chest and putting his hands behind his back. "Good-bye," he said.

"Good-bye," said Jamsir. "Aim!" the rifles came up once more. "Fire!" The five rifles fired simultaneously, and suddenly there were five badly mutilated men bleeding all over the hold.

*   *   *

"They forgot to clean the grease out of the barrels," said Anthony. He was sitting in the saloon clutching a large glass of scotch and shaking like a leaf. "I noticed it earlier on, but I didn't like to mention it."

"Aye," said the Chief in high delight. "Blew Jamsir's head clean off his shoulders. Prettiest sight I've seen for a long time. The others just turned the whole thing in, they were so shattered."

"Well done," said Doyle.

"Very good show," said Ram Singh.

"I knew you couldn't be as stupid as you looked," said McGraw.

Anthony took another long swallow of his drink and started to feel better. He turned to McGraw. "Captain, you told me I was the temporary owner of this ship and that the owner outranked the captain."

"Aye, I told you that. But I don't think . . ."

"I don't much care what you think. Just listen. For the remainder of this voyage I shall eat in my cabin or in the saloon, as I please. But never will I eat lunch with you in your cabin. Neither will I eat curried haggis, nor porridge." He turned to Doyle. "And you, Mister. If you bat your eyelids at me once more, *I* shall throw you overboard myself. Good afternoon, gentlemen."

He climbed to his feet unsteadily, the booze having taken a good hold on him by now. He bowed once to the officers and headed for the door. After a moment of struggling with the handle, he managed to get it open. Then he turned for his parting shot to MacGraw.

"And if I feel like going to bed with the entire crew, I shall do just that."

6

"WHY HAVE WE STOPPED?" ASKED ANTHONY. He was on the bridge, having been summoned there by Wong at four o'clock in the morning. Apart from the helmsman, McGraw and Doyle were also on the bridge. McGraw was wearing his dressing gown and slippers, livid at having been dragged from his bed at the same time as Anthony.

"Mr. Doyle received this signal," said McGraw. "He called me and, because it is none of my concern, I called you."

Anthony took the slip of paper McGraw handed him and read it in the light from the compass housing.

DUE TO INTERNAL TROUBLES PLEASE HEAVE TO TWENTY MILES DUE WEST OF CANSTARTISVILLE STOP POST MASTHEAD LIGHTS AT NIGHT AWAIT ARRIVAL GENERAL DOLIVERA STOP FOLLOW HIS INSTRUCTIONS REFERENCE DELIVERY OF CARGO SIGNED MIGUEL CANSTARTIS PRESIDENT.

"What does it mean?" asked Anthony.

McGraw snorted in disgust. "It means your President is having revolution troubles again. He doesn't want to risk those guns of yours falling into the wrong hands. He's got some special, sneaky orders for unloading them."

"I don't see that it will make much difference," said Anthony.

"It'll mean instead of sailing into a safe harbour in broad daylight, we'll likely have to offload in the middle of the night off a coastline that can take the bottom off a ship before you can say 'homosexual'."

"It may not be like that," said Anthony. "After all, we don't know for sure."

"Take my word for it, young fellow. It will." said McGraw. "Now I'm awa' back to bed." He turned and stalked off the bridge, his dressing-gown flapping dustily behind him.

"Where are we?" Anthony asked Doyle. The mate walked over to the chart table and pointed to his latest plot. "How long do we have to wait here?"

Doyle shrugged. "Until your General Dolivera turns up."

Anthony thought about this for a moment, then he decided that McGraw had the right idea. "I'm going back to bed," he said. "Let me know if anything happens."

"Yes, sir," said Doyle. All the officers, save McGraw, called him "sir" nowadays. Since the mutiny he had been treated with a guarded respect, and the voyage had even

140

become quite pleasant. Wong prepared his food personally, and he ate it where and when he wanted to. When the weather had been fine, which was most of the time, he had spent his days sun-bathing on a section of the deck that had been cleaned and organised for him; a hammock had been slung and cushions had been requisitioned from God knows where; Wong had even managed to keep the fridge working well enough to provide him with a constant supply of ice for his drinks. The three days round the Cape had proved pretty traumatic, everyone except McGraw expecting the *Maria* to take the final plunge to the bottom; but even that had passed and as soon as they had turned north again, the weather started to improve once more. Anthony resumed his long lazy days in the sun, soaking up the vitamins and generally living a life of complete contentment. Now he was as brown as he had ever been and was feeling fitter than he could remember. All the misgivings he'd had about his job had been toasted out of him by the sun and he had found himself silently thanking Walpole, Daddy Henshawe and even Lilian for making the whole thing possible. All he needed to make his life complete was the delectable Shirleen. As he climbed back into bed after his visit to the bridge, he wondered vaguely whether the message from Canastartis would mean trouble; but there was no point in speculation, and two minutes later, he was sound asleep again.

*   *   *

They spent the whole of the following day hove to, waiting for some sort of instructions. But the horizon remained clear and the radio silent.

"I told you," said McGraw, late in the afternoon. "It's

141

something sneaky that can only be done at dead of night. And if we get no word by midnight, I'm sailing straight into Canstartisville and bugger the lot of 'em."

"I shall decide what we shall do, Captain," said Anthony, secure in his newly won authority.

McGraw scowled at him. "Aye. And what will that be?"

"I don't know yet," said Anthony.

"Be sure to let me know when you've made up your mind," said McGraw, striding away and starting to shout at the crew. As it turned out it wasn't necessary for Anthony to make up his mind; at ten-thirty p.m. he was called from his cabin by Wong.

"Captain. He want you on bridge."

"What for?"

"Him say boat coming up."

Anthony ran up on to the bridge to find Doyle and McGraw looking out to port. "Can you no see it, Mister?" McGraw was saying.

"Not a thing, Captain."

"You've no idea what sort of a boat she may be?"

"Not too large by the sound of her."

Anthony joined them. He, too, could see nothing in the darkness, but the sound of the boat's engines came clearly across the water. The three men stood straining their eyes into the night, desperately trying to pick up the first sighting of the approaching vessel. When a spotlight was suddenly turned on, shining directly at them, they were all completely blinded.

"Bloody maniacs!" yelled McGraw, staggering round the bridge bumping into things.

It was a good two minutes before any of them could see

142

again, by which time the approaching boat had bumped hard into the side of the *Maria*, and men were already climbing aboard. McGraw refused to leave the bridge, so Anthony and Doyle went down to greet the arrivals. Four men were standing on the deck, looking around them, not quite sure which way to go. As Anthony and Doyle came towards them, one of them detached himself from the group, took three paces forward, stopped and saluted.

"General Santos Dolivera," he said by way of introduction. He was a tall, very thin man with a sad looking moustache draped across a mouth that looked as though it had been chopped into his face with a *machette*. He was wearing large lensed dark glasses which hid his eyes; his nose was thin and predatory and one of his ears was missing. He was wearing the dark green fatigues so beloved of South American generals, with a matching, baseball style cap. Three stars were pinned to the front of his cap in the form of a triangle and this *motif* was repeated on his shoulder epaulettes.

"How do you do?" said Anthony. "I'm Anthony Bridges and this is Mister Doyle, First Officer of the *Maria*."

The General clicked his heels and bobbed his head. "A pleasure, gentlemen." His English was perfect. "We will start the unloading immediately. We will transfer the guns to my vessel."

Doyle moved to the rail and looked over. "It'll probably take more than one trip, General," he said. "That's not a very large ship."

"We will make as many trips as are necessary."

"Isn't there anywhere we can sail the *Maria* and unload direct?"

"That will be impossible, I'm afraid."

Doyle shrugged. "I'll tell the Captain," he said, turning to go.

"Wait a minute," said Anthony. Both men turned to look at him. "I must send a cable before we start to unload."

"What cable?" said the General.

"My instructions were to cable London. They will cable a reply when it is all right to unload."

"But you are here. I am here. What is the object of contacting London which is seven thousand miles away?"

Anthony felt embarrassed. "It's not my idea," he said. "It's something to do with the payment."

The General smiled. "Ah yes," he said. "But there is no longer any need to send your cable. I have the money right here." He reached behind him and one of his men handed him a leather satchel. He unclipped it, opened the flap and handed the satchel to Anthony. Anthony peered inside. There was a great deal of money there, all in American dollars.

"You will want to count it, of course," said the General. "Meanwhile we will start the unloading." He turned to Doyle. "If you will be kind enough to have your crew start loading in the hold, we can swing the cases straight aboard my vessel where my men will unload them."

Doyle glanced at Anthony who had desperately been trying to make a quick, visual count of the contents of the satchel. "O.K. sir?" he asked.

"Mm?" said Anthony, looking up from the satchel.

"Can we start bringing the stuff up?"

This wasn't at all according to instructions, thought Anthony, but after all he did have the money, and that was all that mattered in the long run. He made up his mind. "Yes. Go ahead Mr. Doyle. I'll go to my cabin and count the money."

"I'll come with you," said the General. He turned and

144

barked a couple of orders to his men, and then turned and followed Anthony.

*   *   *

Before starting to count the money, Anthony asked the General if he wanted a drink, and poured one for himself as well. Then, watched closely by the General, he sat at his small desk and started counting the money. It took him half an hour. Then just to be sure, he started all over again. During the whole time, the General never said a word; he sat across from Anthony, anonymous behind his dark glasses, occasionally getting up to replenish his and Anthony's glasses. Finally Anthony sat back. "Two hundred and seventy thousand dollars," he said. "Exactly right."

"Naturally," said the General. "We are very punctilious."

"Why were the plans changed?" asked Anthony. "I was told that the payment was to be made in Switzerland."

"Foreign currency became available here in Santhoma," said the General. "It seemed less complicated to perform the transaction this way. It makes no difference, I trust?"

"No, none at all," said Anthony, who was just beginning to realise that he now had the responsibility of carrying around more than a quarter of a million dollars in cash. He suddenly started to feel very vulnerable. "I suppose there isn't a bank in Santhoma where I can deposit this and have it transferred to Switzerland?"

"I'm sorry," said the General. "All foreign currency that comes into Santhoma is automatically frozen here."

"Oh," said Anthony. "It seems rather a lot of money to carry around."

"My advice is to sail North to Andestina. There are Swiss banks there. They will handle your money for you. And, after all, there is very little that can happen to it as long as you are aboard the *Maria*."

That's what you think, thought Anthony. "That sounds like a good idea, General," he said, getting to his feet.

"In the meantime why not have the Captain lock it in his safe," said the General, also standing up.

"I think I'll hang on to it."

"As you wish, of course," said the General. "Now we will go and check how they are getting on with the unloading."

"Good idea," said Anthony. They both walked out towards the foredeck. "Sorry to hear you're having internal problems," he went on, to make conversation.

"We are always having internal problems in Santhoma. Though it is my belief that soon they will be coming to an end and Santhoma will be entering a long period of peace and political stability."

"That will be nice for you," said Anthony.

*   *   *

On deck, the transferring of the cargo was going well. The ship's crew were in the hold loading the crates on to the cargo hoist, while the General's men were offloading them direct on to the smaller vessel. Every tenth crate was broken open by one of the General's men and its contents checked. One rifle had been cleaned of all its outside grease and now, as the General arrived on deck, it was handed to him with a loaded magazine. The General hefted it in his hands, then brought it up to his shoulder to fire.

"Excuse me a moment, General," said Anthony quickly.

The General turned to him suspiciously. "You do not wish me to fire the gun?"

146

"It's not that. It's just that the barrels are packed with grease."

"Of course," said the General shortly.

"I just wondered whether your men were aware of it."

"They are soldiers."

"I know that, sir. But wouldn't it be better to take a look. Accidents can happen."

Smiling superciliously, the General ejected that cartridge from the breach, clicked out the bolt expertly and, reversing the rifle, held it up towards one of the deck lights, squinting down the barrel. Then he lowered the rifle and called over the man who had handed it to him. He gave it to the soldier and told him to look through the barrel. While the man was still doing so, the General kicked him hard in the crotch. Later, after half a pound of grease had been removed from the barrel, he tested the shooting action, using it on the man who was still nursing his crotch, thus killing two birds with one stone. Then he turned to Anthony, who was feeling a little sick. You saved my life. *Señor* Bridges."

"It was nothing," said Anthony.

"To you perhaps not. But to me and Santhoma my life is important: we are both grateful."

Anthony, who was still feeling queasy at the casual execution of the unfortunate soldier, nodded politely. "Any time, General."

* * *

Doyle was proved to be wrong; the General's vessel managed to take the entire cargo in one load. Admittedly it overflowed the hold and was piled ten feet high on the entire deck space of the small ship; the Plimsoll line had long since disappeared beneath sea level. But everyone seemed satisfied,

147

and it was just beginning to get light in the East when an officer reported to the General that they were ready to leave. The General shook Anthony's hand warmly and, saluting him, stepped down into his own boat. A moment later the engines started and the heavily overloaded little ship started to wallow away from the *Maria*. Doyle joined Anthony at the rail.

"Anything other than a dead calm and she'll go straight to the bottom," he said, annoyed that his prediction had turned out to be wrong. Anthony looked around him; the sun was coming up on a millpond sea. He decided that the General would have nothing to worry about, and at that moment he felt the engines of the *Maria* start beneath his feet. At the same time he heard his name called.

"Mr. Bridges!" He turned towards the voice. McGraw was leaning over the bridge rail looking towards him. "Could you be sparing me a moment of your valuable time?"

"Watch it!" said Doyle. "The old bastard is after something."

The Captain was smiling when Anthony came up on to the bridge. "That all went very smoothly," said McGraw. "Don't you think?"

"Yes I do," said Anthony.

"That's what comes of running a happy ship. A happy ship is an efficient ship. Don't you agree?"

"I suppose so," said the mystified Anthony.

"And an efficient ship is a real goldmine if she's handled properly." Anthony suddenly realised that he was still carrying the General's satchel. He clutched it a little more firmly. "Have you ever thought of going into the shipping business?" continued McGraw.

"Shipping business?"

"Ship owning. Like Onassis."

"No," said Anthony. "I've never thought about it."

"Do," said the Captain. "Young fellow like you, all that money, you should be thinking of investing for the future."

"It's not mine," said Anthony. "It belongs to the company."

"They'd probably thank you," said McGraw. "No more messing around with charters if they owned their own ship. For a consideration I'd even be willing to discuss staying aboard and running her for you."

"I don't think so," said Anthony.

McGraw shrugged. "Perhaps I am getting a little past it. Not as young as I used to be. Be sorry to see the back of her though. She's been a good old friend these past five years. All right, you're a hard man, but I like you, so I'll take two hundred thousand dollars cash and three hundred thousand over five years at twelve per cent." Anthony shook his head. "Ten per cent over seven years?" Anthony shook his head again. "Seven and a half per cent?"

"I'm not disputing your terms, Captain," said Anthony. "It's just that I'm not authorised by my company to buy any ships right now. Why don't you contact them direct?"

The Captain started to look sulky. "You're missing a grand opportunity."

"That may be," said Anthony. "Now if you will be good enough to drop me off in Andestina, I shall be grateful."

"We're not going to Andestina."

"Where are you going?"

"Chile."

"That will be fine."

"I *could* go to Andestina, but you'd have to pay."

"How much?"

"First class passage? Five thousand dollars should cover it."

"I could go round the world for five thousand dollars."

"Suit yourself," said the Captain.

"All right," said Anthony. "How much to Chile then?"

"Five thousand dollars."

"You mean it's five thousand dollars wherever I go?"

"That's about it," said McGraw.

"And if I refuse to pay you anything?"

As usual the Captain had the last word. "I'll throw you overboard."

*　　　*　　　*

Andestina turned out to be very pleasant for Anthony. And the nicest thing that happened to him was standing on the terrace of his hotel room on the second day, watching the *Maria* put to sea. McGraw had tried to pick up a cargo without success; then he had learned that someone just the other side of the Panama Canal wanted to ship a million pounds of high explosive to Venezuela. He had cabled his quote for the job, received an affirmative reply, and weighed anchor immediately. But by this time Anthony and the *Maria* had parted company, and he only heard about it from Doyle who had come to say goodbye and to borrow a hundred dollars. As soon as the *Maria* had docked Anthony had gone straight to the Swiss Bank, clutching the satchel which he'd not let out of his sight for a single moment. He had deposited the money with instructions that it be forwarded to Hengun's Swiss account. Then he had cabled Walpole telling him what he had done.

That had been two days ago; two days spent by the hotel swimming pool admiring the local talent and wondering how

150

he was going to strike up an acquaintance with one of them. All the girls who were in the least attractive seemed to be watched over by forbidding, sharp-eyed chaperones or by suspicious looking South American gentlemen who looked as though they would pull a knife if Anthony came within fifteen feet of their womenfolk. Added to these more obvious handicaps was the fact that Anthony couldn't speak a word of Spanish, so even if he had been able to get close to any of the girls, his line of chat which served him so well in London would have been quite useless.

On the third day he returned to his room at the end of the afternoon session, feeling more frustrated than ever. He was wearing regulation pool dress, a short towelling robe over his swimming shorts, and carrying a Spanish-English dictionary. He had purchased this from the news-stand in the hotel lobby earlier in the afternoon and had spent the past couple of hours working out the Spanish for "Please can you direct me to the nearest whore house". He believed he had it worked out, and as soon as he was changed he was going to go to the far side of the town, a long way from the hotel, and try it out. He was repeating the phrase to himself under his breath, trying to make it sound casual as well as accurate, as he opened the door to his room and walked in. At once he sniffed an unfamiliar perfume on the air, and almost at the same moment he spotted the girl. She was lying on her side, on the bed, fast asleep, with her back to him. And she was completely naked. At that precise moment she seemed like the most naked girl Anthony had ever seen. Her discarded clothes lay in a pile on the floor beside the bed and there was a veritable mountain of suitcases strewn around the room.

I'm in the wrong room, was Anthony's immediate thought. Backing out quickly, he closed the door quietly and took a deep breath. Then automatically he looked at the number on the door. It was his room all right. He considered for a moment what his next move should be. He could ring down to the desk and ask what a naked girl was doing in his room, or he could march into the room again and wake her up himself. It was a no contest. He took a deep breath, opened the door once more, and marched in.

The girl was still fast asleep on the bed. He went over to take a closer look and decided that from where he was standing she was even more attractive than he had at first assumed. He still couldn't see her face as she had managed to go to sleep with her head half buried beneath the pillow. He supposed he would have to wake her eventually, but first he took very careful inventory of the rest of her. Then, when he could no longer contain the reactions this provoked, he reached out and touched her shoulder gently.

"Excuse me, Señorita," he said. "I'm awfully afraid you are in the wrong room."

The gorgeous creature rolled over on to her back, opened her eyes, brushed the hair back from her face and said, "Well that's an enthusiastic welcome, I must say!"

"Shirleen!" stammered Anthony. "What are you doing here?"

"Looking for a good lay," she said.

*　　　*　　　*

Looking back on it afterwards, Anthony reckoned that it had taken him exactly one-fifth of a second to discard his robe and swim pants. After that there was a gap of something like four hours. When he woke up it was dark outside and Shirleen was sitting up in bed shaking him.

"Shirleen!" he said. "What are you doing here?"

"Not again, darling," she answered. "You're repeating yourself." And as consciousness was restored, he heard her wailing, "I'm hungry."

"You mean you want to . . ." he began, and she said, "No. Not that sort of hungry. I need food and drink. The last square meal I had was in London."

*　　　*　　　*

After they had put on robes and the room service waiter had wheeled in a trolley groaning under the weight of caviar and chicken in aspic and peaches and cheese and champagne, they ate and drank and between mouthfuls Shirleen told Anthony how she came to be lying on his bed.

"It's quite simple really," she said. "You see, when I got back to Hill Street and found your note, I just sat there and blubbed like a baby. And then I said: 'Shirleen, my girl, forget him. He's obviously just another of those fuck-and-run boys. You'll never see him again.' And then I started blubbing all over again because I thought if I didn't see you again I didn't want to go on living and then I said, 'Now you're being childish. Go out and get laid by someone else and you'll feel better.' So I went to the club and I got introduced to this dishy young executive type ram – you know, rugger player, guards' tie, huge shoulders and the rest of the equipment to match, and we went back to his place and he showed me a diamond ring with a stone as big as a plover's egg and said, 'That's for you, baby, if you're as good as you look.' And then he undressed me and all that and then – you'll never believe this, but it's true, as God is my witness – I couldn't do it. I just could *not* do it. I put all my things back on and I gave him back his diamond ring and I patted his

153

equipment and told him it was fabulous but not for me and I rushed out of the place as though a shipful of sailors was after me. It's no good, Anthony, a terrible thing has happened to me. I can only do it with you. I know it's kooky, but it's true. You're my dish and as far as I'm concerned you're the grooviest thing in the world and you have exclusive rights."

Anthony kissed her. "I'm not complaining."

"Of course I may get over it when I'm an old woman, like twenty-three or four, but for the moment you have me on a string. You're my dish – the grooviest dish in the world . . ." She looked across at him appealingly. "You didn't mind me following you out here and going to sleep on your bed without being asked?"

"Not at all. But how did you manage to find me?"

"I went down and blackmailed Daddy Henshawe. He didn't want to tell me at first and he hated having to pay for my air ticket, but I remembered one or two things I'd heard when I was his sexatary and when I repeated them to him he gave in." She leaned back in her chair and stretched luxuriously. "That was absolutely fab, darling. You know what? I think I'd like to start all over again. How about you?"

"You go ahead if you want to, but I couldn't eat another mouthful."

"I wasn't talking about eating, darling. At least, not food."

*　　　*　　　*

It was nearly noon before Anthony tottered out of the elevator and crossed to the reception desk to make arrangements for Shirleen and himself to be moved into a larger suite. The clerk couldn't have been more helpful and Anthony quickly found himself possessed of the best suite in the hotel with a balcony overlooking the pool. Thank God for expense accounts, he told himself.

While all this was being arranged he glanced idly at the front page of the pile of local newspapers lying on the desk. The paper was printed in Spanish and Anthony didn't understand a word of it, but he did recognise the picture on the front page. It was General Dolivera.

Turning the paper around so that it faced the clerk, he asked him what the headlines said.

"There has been another revolution in Santhoma," the man told him.

"Oh dear! That's General Dolivera, isn't it?" Anthony asked, pointing at the picture.

"It is indeed," said the clerk.

"What happened to him?" asked Anthony. "Was he beheaded in the main square, or did they shoot him?"

The clerk looked at him in astonishment. "But, sir, General Dolivera is the new President. May I read the item to you?"

"Please do," said Anthony, with a sinking feeling.

The clerk's English was accented but good—and there was no doubt about what he was reading: "The revolutionary army under the command of General Santos Dolivera has emerged victorious in the recent power struggle in Santhoma. The former President, Miguel Canstartis, is believed to have fled the country and General Dolivera has declared himself President and commander in chief of the armed forces. His small army, only ten thousand strong, was remarkably well armed for a revolutionary group; experts say that this fact was the main cause of the success of his uprising."

That's torn it, thought Anthony. I've sold the guns to the wrong side!

*   *   *

155

"If you'd followed instructions this would never have happened," said Walpole. The line to London was very bad and Anthony had trouble in understanding everything that Walpole was saying. But the basic content was coming through loud and clear. Walpole was seriously displeased.

"You got the money, didn't you?" asked Anthony.

"Certainly we got the money. That's not the point. Miguel Canstartis was an old and valued client."

"Perhaps Dolivera will turn out the same way," said Anthony hopefully.

"Let us indeed hope so," said Walpole. It was amazing how cold he could make his voice sound over seven thousand odd miles of telephone wire. "I suggest you find out."

"How do you mean?"

"Go to Santhoma and ask Dolivera what he needs."

"But he's just won a revolution. Why should he need guns ow?"

"That's up to you to find out. And if you can't sell him anything, I suggest you try to locate Canstartis. He will most certainly be in need of guns right now."

"He's not going to like me very much though," said Anthony.

"Then that will make two of us," said Walpole; and he hung up.

*   *   *

But there was one person who liked Anthony very much and, because of her, he left it another couple of days before starting back to work. Then he sent a tentative cable direct to President Dolivera and sat back, not really expecting a reply. Dolivera's answer arrived the following day; not in the form of a cable, but a visit from the Santhomese Ambassador.

156

Señor Alvira was a fat little man whose natural pomposity had become severely deflated during the last few days. As Ambassador appointed by Canstartis, he was expecting the chop to come from Dolivera hourly. There had been an ominous silence from the new regime, only broken by the telex message concerning Anthony. As far as Alvira was concerned, any orders from the new President meant that his job was safe, at least for the time being, and so Anthony had assumed the proportions of a saviour in the Ambassador's eyes. He bowed himself into the suite as though he were approaching the throne of God Almighty and Anthony, who had just been for a swim and was still wearing wet bathing trunks, suddenly felt ridiculously underdressed. Alvira had dressed for the occasion in full ambassadorial regalia, complete to plumed, three-cornered hat, red sash, and blazingly obscure jewelled stars scattered all over his fat little chest and stomach.

"*Señor* Bridges, it is an honour for me to present myself to you on behalf of our great *Presidente,* Santos Dolivera."

"How do you do?" said Anthony. At that moment, Shirleen appeared from the bedroom, wearing only the bottom half of her bikini. Wherever it was that Alvira had learned his diplomacy, he had learned it well; he didn't bat an eyelid as he bowed low.

"*Señora,*" he said.

"*Señorita,*" said Shirleen, equally unabashed.

"A thousand million pardons, *Señorita,*" said Alvira. "For a lady as beautiful and gracious as yourself it was unthinkable that she should still be unmarried."

Shirleen flashed her beautiful teeth at him. "You're very sweet," she said. Then she turned to Anthony. "I was going

157

to ask you to bring me a drink, darling. I'm sorry, I didn't know you were busy."

"Please," begged Alvira. "Nothing could be as important as your well being, *Señorita*." Shirleen smiled at him once more and returned to the bedroom.

"Excuse me a moment," said Anthony. He poured her drink and carried it through to her.

"Who's that darling little man so full of shit?" she asked.

"The Santhomese Ambassador."

"What on earth does he want with you?"

"I'll let you know when he tells me," said Anthony dragging on a towelling robe. He walked back into the sitting room. Alvira, who had sat down, now sprang to his feet again.

"Please," said Anthony. "Don't get up."

Alvira ignored him. "*Señor* Bridges. I have been instructed by *el Presidente* Dolivera to extend to you his personal invitation to visit our fair country. If you are agreeable, *el Presidente* will send his own personal aircraft here to transport you there in the style befitting your excellency's status."

"Thanks very much," said Anthony.

Alvira looked a little surprised. "You accept?"

"Of course," said Anthony.

Alvira had been expecting a battle; as far as he knew nobody ever wanted to go to Santhoma. But he covered up well. "Yes, of course you accept. It was just that for a man of your importance . . . Well, so many other things to occupy his time and attention; I didn't think you would be so . . . so readily available." He desperately wanted to find out just who and what Anthony was, in case he could use the knowledge later. "A man in your position . . . affairs to settle . . ." He tailed off, realising that unless Anthony volunteered the information, he was going to learn nothing. In fact, if he had

158

come right out and asked, Anthony would have told him. But Alvira didn't know this any more than Anthony knew what Alvira was fishing for.

"When do we go?" asked Anthony.

"I shall cable Santhoma immediately. The *Presidente's* aircraft will arrive tomorrow morning at the latest."

"Fine," said Anthony. "One other thing. I suppose it will be all right if I take the *Señorita* along?"

"Of course. Of course," said Alvira, who really had no idea. "I will send the embassy car here to the hotel at noon tomorrow." He drew himself up to his full five feet four inches and bowed again. "It has been an extreme honour, *Señor* Bridges. I trust that you will give *el Presidente* my very best wishes, assuring him at the same time of my unswerving loyalty and devotion."

"Certainly," said Anthony, walking to the door with Alvira.

"I envy you, Mr. Bridges. Would that I could gaze once more on the land of my birth."

"Why don't you come with us?" suggested Anthony. "I'm sure there'll be plenty of room in the plane."

"If *el Presidente* wants me he will send for me," said Alvira. Actually he had no intention of going anywhere near Santhoma until things settled down and he knew exactly where he stood with the new regime; until that time he felt a lot safer almost anywhere else in the world.

They reached the door and Anthony opened it, allowing Alvira to walk past him. "Well, thanks for calling," he said. Alvira bowed once more and, breathing a sigh of relief at having accomplished his task, scuttled back to the security of the Embassy.

Anthony went through into the bedroom. "We're going to

Santhoma tomorrow," he said to Shirleen, who was sitting at the dressing table brushing her hair.

"Is that what he wanted?" she asked.

Anthony nodded. "The President is sending his personal plane for us."

"That'll be nice," said Shirleen, apparently completely unimpressed.

Anthony felt a twinge of disappointment; he badly wanted to impress her and, if he couldn't do it with a President's aeroplane, then he would have to resort to more intimate methods. Not that he saw very much wrong with that. He stood close behind her as she sat in front of the mirror, and slid his hands under her arms until each hand held one of her breasts. Shirleen stopped brushing and started to purr.

*   *   *

Later that morning Anthony booked a telephone call to Walpole in London. It came through in the middle of dinner, and Walpole wasn't at all pleased because it was the middle of the night where he was and he let Anthony know vividly that he didn't approve of being wakened from his sleep. Anthony waited patiently while Walpole worked off his initial foul temper and as soon as he saw an opportunity he slipped in his first remark. "I'm going to Santhoma tomorrow."

"So?"

"So I'm going to try to sell Dolivera more guns."

"That's what you're overpaid for."

"Trouble is, I don't know what guns we've got available, or how much to ask for them."

"We've got whatever he wants."

"Really?"

"Just get his order and tell me what it is.'

"What about price?"

"Tell him you'll settle the price later. Ask for Ramirez to act as intermediary; he knows how to deal with them."

"Carlos Ramirez?"

"How many Ramirezes do you know?"

"Just Carlos."

"Exactly. Anything else?"

Anthony was sure there were a dozen things, but he couldn't think of any of them. "No, sir," he said, and the line went dead. Anthony checked with the operator who told him that it wasn't a broken connection but that his party had hung up the phone the other end. So up you too, thought Anthony, and went back to his dinner.

*   *   *

That night was one of Shirleen's gala performances and Anthony was feeling exhausted, but full of euphoria, as he went downstairs to pay the bill. He was walking back to the elevator counting his change when somebody spoke to him from just behind his left shoulder. "Mr. Bridges?" He turned and nearly bumped into two men who were right behind him. One was very tall and thin with the largest adam's apple he had ever seen; the other was short, also thin, with the completely anonymous sort of face one sees in insurance advertisements. Both were neatly dressed in dark blue suits, blue button down shirts and blue neckties. They looked like a couple of advertising men on vacation from Madison Avenue.

"Yes?" said Anthony. "I'm Bridges."

"Harvey Dacron," said the taller of the two men.

"Stanley Parsons," said the shorter.

"How do you do?" said Anthony. "Are you from the Embassy?"

The two men flashed a look at one another, then Dacron turned back to Anthony. "How did you know?"

"I was expecting you," said Anthony. "But you're early."

"You were?" said Dacron.

"We are?" said Parsons.

"The Ambassador said about midday."

"You've talked to the Ambassador?"

"Of course," said Anthony. "It was his idea."

The two men looked at one another again. "What's the old coot up to?" asked Dacron.

"Search me," said Parsons.

"Washington?" asked Dacron.

"Definitely," said Parsons. And without another word the two men turned and walked off across the lobby towards the main entrance. Anthony watched them go; then with a shrug he turned and continued towards the elevators.

*   *   *

Shirleen's suitcases – he was amazed to note that there were eleven of them – were stacked in the living room when he came in; to one side of this opulent pile of matched luggage were his two strictly functional, badly scuffed suitcases, carrying the scars of Lamboola and the *Maria*. Shirleen was in the bedroom putting the final touches to her already immaculate person. Anthony decided that she looked like a fresh spring day in Paris; he was so pleased with this thought that he told her. She smiled at him and kissed him. One thing led to another and she had to repair her make-up before he was able to answer the telephone, which had been ringing for at least ten minutes. It was the reception desk to tell him that

162

the Embassy car was waiting. Anthony glanced at Shirleen's luggage.

"How many cars?" he asked.

"Just one, *señor.*" Anthony ordered two taxis to accompany them to the airport and told the desk to send up every available bellboy to collect the luggage. Then he escorted Shirleen to the elevator.

*   *   *

The Embassy Mercedes drove them out to the airport where its diplomatic plates carved a wide swathe through the customs and immigration. The Presidential aircraft was waiting at the end of the runway and the car drove straight to it. Perhaps this will impress Shirleen, he thought, but one look at her calm placid expression and he doubted it. Two minutes after their arriving aboard, the engines revved up and they were off. As they sped down the runway, building up speed, Anthony glanced out of the window. The two taxis containing all their luggage were just pulling up at the take-off apron.

*   *   *

"It doesn't matter, dreamboat. Honestly!" said Shirleen for the tenth time. "Either they'll send it or you can buy me new stuff. It's not important – just so long as I have one nightie for you to tear off me."

The Presidential aircraft was a Boeing 727; the interior had been designed for a maximum occupancy of five. There was one large cabin which served as sitting room, dining room, office, etcetera, and behind a midway bulkhead were three bedrooms each with its own bathroom. The two stewardesses were very pretty and extremely efficient and, halfway through the flight, the Captain came back to present his

163

compliments and ask how they were enjoying the trip. Anthony pulled himself together sufficiently to smile at the Captain, but that man was so enchanted with Shirleen that he wouldn't really have noticed if Anthony had grown another head. In fact he stayed so long chatting with her that Anthony started to get annoyed all over again.

"Who's tending the store?" he asked finally.

"I'm sorry," said the Captain turning reluctantly from Shirleen. "What did you say, sir?"

"I said who's flying this thing while you're back here socialising?"

The Captain wasn't disturbed. "My first officer is very competent. You don't have to concern yourself."

"I'll mention that to the President," said Anthony. "He'll be glad to hear it."

That got through to the Captain. He saluted politely and went back to the flight deck.

"That was rather rude, wasn't it?" said Shirleen.

"I was jealous."

"No need to be. When the time comes for you to be jealous you'll know because I shall tell you."

Oh shit, thought Anthony. This just isn't my day. "I'm sorry," he said.

"Apologies accepted," said Shirleen, rather grandly. Then she smiled at him. "Now let's enjoy ourselves. It's not every day I get to travel on a President's private aircraft. It really is very groovy. You must be a very important man indeed." At that moment the sun came out for Anthony and he really did start to enjoy himself. The stewardess opened another bottle of champagne and then served them lunch. They had hardly finished their brandy when the Captain's voice came

164

over the public address asking them to attach their seat belts as they started their descent towards Santhoma.

*   *   *

The first thing Anthony noticed was a gang of workmen painting out the name Canstartisville on the airport terminal building; they were working from left to right and already the name Doliveraville was beginning to take shape. The aircraft taxied to a dispersal point and, by the time the gangway was in place, there was a car waiting at the bottom. A nervous young man was waiting for them, sweating and cracking his knuckles with a sound like breaking twigs.

"I am *Señor* Granada," he said. "*El Presidente* presents his compliments and apologises that he is unable to meet you personally. He has instructed me to escort you to the palace."

Anthony told Granada about the mishap with the baggage and he promised to take care of it. Then he escorted them into the car and fussed around like a mother hen making them comfortable. The chauffeur was wearing green battle fatigues and, sitting next to him in the front, was another soldier nursing a sub-machine gun. As the car picked up speed heading out of the airport, there was a scream of sirens and suddenly, as though from nowhere, they had an escort of a dozen motor-cycles, ridden by as villainous a looking bunch, all heavily armed, as Anthony had ever seen.

"Hell's angels," said Shirleen.

"I'm glad they're on our side," said Anthony. Then he turned to Granada. "They *are* on our side. I suppose?" he asked with a smile.

Granada didn't smile. "Oh yes. Have no fear. They are *el Presidente's* personal bodyguard."

165

"I was joking," said Anthony quietly to Shirleen.

"He wasn't," she replied.

*   *   *

The drive to the palace took thirty minutes. Looking out of the car window, Anthony's main impression was one of intense military activity. Soldiers swarmed everywhere, pulling down barricades, putting up barricades, patrolling roof tops and street corners, even directing traffic.

"Are you expecting trouble?" asked Shirleen innocently after twenty minutes.

Granada's expression grew even more nervous. "Here in Santhoma we are always expecting trouble." Then he realised that he might have made a gaffe. "Of course, with the new *Presidente* we are entering a period of peaceful prosperity,"

"It doesn't look like it," said Anthony. "It looks as though you're entering a period of outright warfare."

Granada cracked his knuckles furiously. "They are clearing up the debris left after the fighting, during which the tyrant Miguel Constartis was finally overcome by the victorious armies of our beloved Santos Dolivera."

"What happened to Canstartis?"

"He escaped. But rest assured he will be apprehended and brought before the courts to answer for the crimes he has committed against the people and the state of Santhoma."

"Amen," said Anthony.

*   *   *

The palace occupied the North side of the main square. It was a large, whitish building with windows facing out across a small courtyard on to the square. It was surrounded by a high wall, the top of which was liberally scattered with broken glass and barbed wire. In the square, gangs of workmen were busy changing the street signs so that they now read Plaza Dolivera. The area in front of the palace gates was filled by a solid phalanx of soldiers, some in outdated armoured cars, but most of them standing around in small groups talking and smoking. They all wore olive green battle dress, and Anthony noticed that all of them carried short magazine Lee Enfields. The gates to the palace opened in front of the car and they swept through. More soldiers were distributed around the courtyard fronting the palace. None of them took any notice of the car or its outriders as the whole procession drew up outside the main entrance. Granada jumped out and held the door open for Anthony and Shirleen. At the same time a man came down from the palace to greet them. He, too, was a soldier and Anthony vaguely recalled having seen his face on board the *Maria*. He threw Anthony a brisk salute.

"Colonel Guardino at your service," he said. "*El Presidente* has asked that you be brought to him the moment that you have arrived."

Shirleen was handed over to the care of Granada and Anthony followed the Colonel along corridors and up stairs, past a great many more soldiers, to the President's ante-room. This, too, was lined with soldiers, but also contained a large number of very nervous looking civilians, most of them clutching briefcases.

"The civil service," explained Guardino contemptuously. "They're all nervous wrecks trembling over their pensions." He said it loudly, not caring who heard, and Anthony decided that he didn't much like Colonel Guardino. At the Colonel's approach, two soldiers, guarding the double doors at the far side of the room, threw them open and Anthony and the Colonel were ushered through. Santos Dolivera was seated behind a large desk at the far end of a sixty-five foot room. His booted feet were resting on the desk and he was smoking a large cigar. Three men stood on the opposite side of the desk. They were engaged in presenting some sort of petition, which didn't seem to be going down at all well with the President. As soon as he saw Anthony, he removed the cigar from his mouth, waved it at the men and snapped something to them that Anthony didn't understand. Without a word, they gathered up their papers and crept out of the room, their eyes glued to the floor. Dolivera took his feet from the desk and stood up.

"*Señor* Bridges. It is a pleasure to see you again so soon." He shook hands and ushered Anthony to a chair. Guardino remained hovering in the background. "First I must apologise for the deception I practised on you," said Dolivera. "But I needed those guns badly." He waved his hand round the office expansively. "You can see why."

What the hell did one say to a newly created President, thought Anthony.

"Congratulations," he said finally.

"Thank you," said Dolivera. "They are deserved. The fighting was bloody. But thanks to you, we overcame. And as one of my first official acts I take great pleasure in presenting you with the Star of Santhoma, second class, for services to the cause of freedom." He beckoned to Guardino, who picked up a broad red sash with a brilliant jewelled star pinned to it. It was on a side table with a couple of dozen similar decorations and Anthony recalled having seen at least six others being worn by various of the soldiers who were patrolling the palace. Guardino handed it to Dolivera who brought it across to Anthony. Anthony stood up and the President placed the sash over his head. Then he kissed him heartily on both cheeks.

"Thank you very much," said Anthony, slightly overwhelmed. After all, he had been conned into making a deal that he'd no intention of making, and now the con man was making him a national hero, second class. Perhaps it wasn't going to be so very difficult to sell him some more guns after all. And now was as good a time as he would get to start his sales pitch.

"Sir . . ." he started.

But Dolivera didn't let him continue. He cut in without even noticing that Anthony wanted to say something. "AR 10s," he said.

"I beg your pardon?"

"I want ten thousand AR 10s. Two hundred light machine guns, twenty-five Cossack armoured cars, twenty light anti-tank guns, two hundred tons of napalm, two hundred tons of nerve gas, and a frigate."

"What sort of a frigate?" It was the only thing Anthony could think of to say.

"Armed, of course. I need it to protect my coastal waters. When can you deliver?"

Anthony, who was rapidly trying to imagine what the total cost of this lot would be and how much one per cent would work out at, but had lost his way after the first couple of million, temporised. "I'll have to consult with London."

"Do that," said Dolivera. "But tell them that time is of the essence. Urgency is paramount."

"Yes, sir."

"Is there anything I can do to assist you in expediting this matter?" asked Dolivera.

Anthony suddenly remembered his last conversation with Walpole. "Do you know a man named Carlos Ramirez?"

"I know him," said Dolivera. "What about him?"

"He would be a great help to me. I'd like him to work as my assistant during the transaction."

Dolivera glanced at Colonel Guardino and said something to him that Anthony didn't understand. The Colonel nodded and left the office quickly. Dolivera turned back to Anthony. "I hope we are in time," he said.

"In time for what?"

"He was due to be executed this afternoon."

"Carlos?" said Anthony, astonished. "What on earth for?"

"He negotiated the purchase of ten thousand rifles for the traitor Miguel Canstartis."

"But you were the one who got the rifles."

"Ramirez didn't know that. Anyway, my friend, providing we're not too late, Ramirez now has a new lease on life."

*   *   *

As it turned out, they were in time, but only just. Executions had been going on all day at the police barracks about half a mile from the palace; around about four o'clock the firing squad had become bored and knocked off for a short rest and a couple of drinks. They were just about to start work again, with Carlos Ramirez first on the list, when he was plucked practically from beneath the barrels of the rifles that he had negotiated for in London. He was taken home and allowed to shave and clean himself up; then he was escorted back to the Palace and straight up to the suite of rooms occupied by Anthony and Shirleen. As soon as Carlos saw Anthony, he fell into his arms, tears in his eyes, his voice choked with emotion.

170

"My old, old friend. You are saving my life. I thank you; my mother thanks you; my father thanks you. My wife and babies thank you; all the Ramirez family are thanking you from the bottoms of their heart." He pushed Anthony to arm's length and looked up at him, his eyes still brimming with tears. "My friend. My *campadre* for life," he said with great solemnity. Then his eyes seemed to dry up miraculously and he was his old self once more. "To business," he said. "You have contacted your Mr. Walpole?"

"Not yet."

"We must do so with the uttermost haste. You have the order list from that bandit Dolivera?"

"I've got it here," said Anthony, fetching it from the desk.

Carlos took the list and read it through quickly; then again more slowly. "It's a formidable list," he said finally.

"That's what I thought."

"Have prices been discussed?"

"Not yet."

"It is better to agree on them right at the start."

"How can I agree prices? I don't even know what an AR 10 is, let alone what it costs."

"I will make an estimation of the prices. Then you can tell the President, God rot him, that we are negotiating."

"If you say so," said Anthony, way out of his depth.

"*Si,*" said Carlos, very businesslike now. "Carlos is saying so."

He went over to the desk and located some scrap paper. Then he started to make some notes. Anthony watched him for a few minutes; after which, growing bored, he walked across to one of the large windows that overlooked the palace courtyard and the main square beyond. The soldiers had rigged up floodlights covering every corner of the square,

171

so that it would have been impossible for anyone to move out there without being plainly visible. Not that there was anybody about, apart from the soldiers. Anthony turned back to Carlos.

"Do you realise I've been here all day and I haven't seen one single solitary Santhomese citizen. Just soldiers and civil servants."

"There's a curfew," said Carlos, without looking up from his calculations.

"I know that," said Anthony. "But before, when we were driving from the airport. Just soldiers."

Carlos turned from his work. "Do you know what the Santhomese man is doing right now? He is meeting with his friends in their houses, and he is plotting."

"Plotting what?"

"The downfall of Dolivera."

"I thought Canstartis was the villain."

"They plotted *his* downfall last week. This week it is Dolivera." He returned to his calculations and two minutes later he had finished. "We will offer you thirty-seven million dollars for what we are asking you to supply."

"We?"

"Of course we. I am the intermediary. Is that not why you asked for me?"

"Certainly. But you're supposed to be on my side."

"I am on your side. We will offer thirty-seven million; you will ask for forty-five. I shall say thirty-eight; you will ask for forty-three. Eventually we will settle for forty million. You will make four hundred thousand dollars, of which you will give me one hundred thousand. Hengun will make two, perhaps three million, and Dolivera will get his arms. Everybody is therefore happy."

172

Carlos had lost Anthony halfway through this speech; after he had said that Anthony would make four hundred thousand dollars, Anthony hadn't heard a word.

"It is all right, my friend?" asked Carlos after a moment when Anthony still hadn't said anything.

"Certainly," said Anthony. "Yes. Fine, just fine."

"Good," said Carlos. "Now all we are having to do is to get hold of the arms That, of course is your job."

"I'll call Walpole," said Anthony.

* * *

He wasn't able to call Walpole because, since the revolution, most of the telephone wires in Santhoma were down, so he settled for sending him a cable which Guardino had to arrange for him because all communications were in the hands of the military. The cable set out the requirements together with the prices that Anthony and Carlos had agreed on. The rest was up to Walpole and, feeling tired and well satisfied with his day's work, Anthony followed Shirleen into bed.

* * *

They were awakened at three in the morning. Anthony groped his way up out of sleep to find the lights on and Colonel Guardino standing in the doorway.

"*El Presidente* wants to see you," he said.

Anthony glanced at his watch. "Now?"

"Immediately."

He started to get out of bed and Shirleen mumbled something at him, still half asleep. He patted her bottom beneath the bedclothes and told her to go back to sleep, then grabbed his clothes and carried them through into the sitting room to

173

get dressed. Guardino followed him, switching off the bedroom light and closing the door quietly behind him. In three minutes, Anthony was dressed and following the Colonel down the corridors to the President's office. The anteroom was empty except for soldiers and, as before, he and Guardino went straight through into the main office. A man looked up from behind the President's desk as they came in. Anthony didn't know who he was, but sure as hell he wasn't Santos Dolivera.

"Good morning, *Señor* Bridges," said the man. "I am Miguel Canstartis."

7

THE OFFICIAL INTERPRETER WAS VERY GOOD AT
his job. He translated everything that was said with exactly
the intonation used by the speaker. If the speaker cleared his
throat or blew his nose in mid-sentence, the interpreter would
do likewise.

"Anthony Bridges," he said. "You have been found guilty
of giving aid to the revolutionary forces in their attempt to
overthrow the legal Government of Santhoma. Have you
anything to say before sentence is passed?"

Anthony had already said it a hundred times, but he tried
again. "I'm not guilty."

The interpreter duly translated this, then sat down while

175

the judge read the sentence. Then he stood up once more and translated what the judge had just said.

"Anthony Bridges, it is my extreme pleasure to sentence you for the crime of which you have been found guilty. You will be executed by hanging in public one week from this date at noon exactly. And may God have mercy on your wicked, evil soul."

Anthony was escorted down to the cell below the courts once more and locked in. His lawyer, appointed by the court, came down to say good-bye to him and to make sure that his fee had been deposited in the local bank. Anthony hadn't liked the lawyer from the start, but up to now he had been reasonably polite, because, after all, the man was supposed to be defending him and there didn't seem to be any point in upsetting him unduly. But now that was all over, and Anthony told him something he had been dying to for a week. "Go fuck yourself," he said.

Señor Alvarez was a small, punctilious man, and his grasp of the English language wasn't as good as it might have been. "What is this 'go fuck yourself'?" he asked with a polite little smile.

Anthony tried putting it another way, and still he didn't manage to get through. But it wasn't going to make any difference, so finally he contented himself with telling Alvarez to leave him alone. After the lawyer had left, he sat down on his bunk and wondered if he would feel any better if he had a good cry. It had all happened so bloody fast, he still wasn't quite sure how he had managed to wind up where he was right now. It seemed that the defeat of Canstartis hadn't been so much of a defeat as a strategic withdrawal. Two days after Dolivera had assumed power, Canstartis had started to

176

contact various elements of Dolivera's army from his hide-out in the hills. His main point of contact had been through Colonel Guardino, Dolivera's right hand, and now a full blown General. And when Guardino told Canstartis that the time was right, Canstartis moved back down from the hills and quietly reoccupied the palace, while Dolivera's men looked the other way. Dolivera had managed to escape through the back door and now *he* had retreated to the hills, there to start plotting the whole thing all over again.

* * *

Apart from that first early morning summons, Anthony hadn't seen Canstartis again. But he still recalled the scene vividly. His first impression of Canstartis had been the sheer physical size of the man. He was about six feet four inches tall and built like a battleship. Unlike everyone else he had seen, Canstartis was not wearing olive green fatigues, but was dressed in a beautifully cut uniform without rank or insignia other than a small row of medal ribbons on his left breast. His eyes were brown and colder than any brown eyes had a right to be. He had a full moustache drooping over his upper lip, and his teeth, when he showed them, were large and very white. He was showing them when Anthony had been shown in, but his smile contained no amusement whatsoever.

"I trust you find your quarters in my palace to your liking?" he had said smoothly.

"Yes, thank you," said Anthony.

"I'm sorry that you won't be able to remain."

"I was leaving anyway," said Anthony.

"Really?"

"General Dolivera ordered some . . ." He stopped; perhaps

177

now wasn't a good time to mention what Dolivera had wanted. Canstartis had continued to smile; the only difference now was that he was beginning to look genuinely amused.

"Carry on, Mr. Bridges," he said. When Anthony didn't continue, he stopped smiling. "I have arranged accommodation for you elsewhere," he said. "Your trial starts on Monday."

"Trial? What trial?"

"You are charged with subversion, treason, murder and rape."

"I didn't murder or rape anyone," said Anthony.

Canstartis smiled once more. "Then we'll just make it subversion and treason," he said.

*   *   *

Anthony had been moved to police headquarters without even being allowed to go back to his rooms to see Shirleen. And all subsequent queries by him as to her whereabouts or well-being were met with stony silence. But at least she hadn't been stood up in court beside him, which was some consolation. The trial had been quick and efficient and he hadn't understood a word except what they wanted him to. This had amounted to the charge and, later, the verdict and sentence. The rest of the time the court didn't allow the interpreter to interrupt the proceedings long enough to interpret. It had lasted two boring days for Anthony, who had spent most of the time searching the courtroom for a familiar face. He had spotted Carlos once, but his smile of recognition had gone unanswered by the little South American. On the evening of the second day Alvarez, his lawyer, had explained to him how things were going.

"Badly," he said.

178

"But I didn't do anything."

"You sold guns to the rebels."

"I didn't know they were rebels."

"That would not be sufficient to get you off, even if it were true."

"It is true."

"Perhaps; perhaps not. It is not important."

"What is important?" asked Anthony desperately.

Alvarez drew himself up dramatically. "That you die like a man," he had pronounced sonorously. With a defence lawyer like this one, Anthony thought, who needed a prosecutor?

*   *   *

And now it was over and he had seven days in which to set his affairs in order before taking the long midday drop. He asked for writing paper and a pen and sat down and wrote some letters. He wrote to his mother and father first, explaining what had happened and what was about to happen. As he read it through, he visualised the scene in the vicarage when it arrived.

"Who's it from, dearest?" his mother would say.

"Anthony."

"How is he?"

"He says he's going to be hanged next week."

"Oh dear. I hope he wraps up well."

His father would immediately rewrite his sermon, bringing in bits about just retribution, the Will of God, the punishment of evildoers, and deliver it to his non-existent congregation the following Sunday.

He wrote to Shirleen, addressing it to her at the Presidential Palace, hoping that they would forward it on to whatever

179

woman's prison she happened to be in right now. In it, he apologised for getting her into trouble and said, if they'd let her out, perhaps she would care to come to the hanging next week. He said that he loved her and that he had been going to ask her to marry him, and that he was sure that they would have been deliriously happy, well into their dotage. He cried a little over this letter, making sure the tears fell on to the paper, smudging the ink, so that she would know he meant what he was saying. And after that he couldn't think of another soul to write to. There didn't seem much point in dropping a note to Walpole; he would know what had happened and would have insulated himself behind paragraph twelve of the service contract. "If the party of the second part is arrested, apprehended, taken prisoner, brought into custody; and if as a result of the aforementioned he is subsequently brought before a Court of Law, military or civilian, howsoever convened, then the party of the first part will disclaim and/or disavow any knowledge of the party of the second part." So up yours, Mr. Walpole, thought Anthony.

*　　*　　*

He had long ago given up any hope of contacting the British Embassy in Santhoma. Indeed, he wasn't even sure that one existed. So he was agreably surprised when, two days after the trial, he received a visitor. Mr. Beamish was about twenty-six years old and looked thirty-nine. He had a tired, sad face, a parchment-like complexion and a bad head cold. He shuffled into Anthony's cell reluctantly and sat himself down on the only chair.

"Don't come too near me, old man," he said. "You'll catch my cold."

180

"They're hanging me this week," said Anthony. "I don't think it'll matter."

"I say, you haven't got any paper hankies, have you?" asked Beamish. "They're hell to get hold of in Doliveraville."

"It's Canstartisville again," said Anthony.

"So it is," said Beamish, trying to sniff some air into his blocked nasal passages.

"Are you going to get me out?" asked Anthony.

"Can't do that, old man," said Beamish. "Her Majesty's Government has disowned you. Can't have HMG consorting with known gunrunners. Bad for the image."

"Fuck the image," said Anthony with some heat. "I don't want to hang."

"Should have thought of that before you started peddling armaments. You haven't got a clean handkerchief you won't be needing, have you?"

"I'm a British citizen," said Anthony. "I have a British passport."

"It's been revoked," said Beamish, without rancour.

"You can't just revoke a passport."

"Yes we can, old man. We've just done it."

"If there's nothing you can do, what did you come to see me about?"

"To tell you about the passport," said Beamish. "And to warn you that it is an offence to travel without one."

"Thank you," said Anthony. "I'll take care."

"Do that," said Beamish getting to his feet. "Must go now, the Under Secretary is giving a cocktail party."

"Just a minute! What are you doing about Miss Jones?"

"Which Miss Jones?"

"Shirleen Jones. The girl who was with me when I was arrested."

"Nobody's told us anything about a girl. Was she arrested, too?"

"I don't know, but it's up to you to find out. And pretty damned quick."

"Was she travelling on a British passport?"

"I think so, yes."

"Don't you know?"

"Not for sure."

"You say *Miss* Jones. I presume she was not married?"

"No. But we were engaged. And I demand to know what has happened to her."

"I'll look into it," said Beamish. "But if she's been consorting with you I expect we shall revoke her passport, too. You can rest assured we shall let her know if we do."

He let go an enormous sneeze and snuffled his way out of the cell. Anthony heard him ask the guard whether he had any paper handkerchiefs.

*　　*　　*

After that, there seemed nothing to do but wait for the hanging. Apparently Santhomese prisons did not believe in cosseting condemned prisoners; there were no special meals and no friendly guard to play chess with. Neither did they take his belt away from him or keep the lights on twenty-four hours a day. As far as they were concerned, if he wanted to hang himself, he was welcome. From the look of the guards, Anthony decided that they would probably come into his cell and help him up on to the stool if he asked them. He tried feigning illness in the hope that they wouldn't want to hang a sick man; but they didn't even call a doctor, and the guards ate the food that he pretended he didn't want. So, sick of lying in bed and eating soap to make his mouth foam,

182

he gave up and, instead, started to exercise ferociously, paying particular attention to the muscles of his neck; if he built them up strong enough, perhaps the rope would break and they would decide that Divine Providence had intervened and let him go. They hadn't allowed him any cigarettes, and he realised after five days that he didn't miss them any longer. This, combined with the exercise and the complete absence of booze, soon had him feeling fitter than he had for the past twenty years. Each day he would be allowed a couple of hours in a small exercise yard; but he didn't appreciate this as much as he might have done due to the almost constant rattle of musketry from somewhere close by, where Canstartis' firing squad were cleaning house for their President.

Before he really knew it, he awoke one morning to the realisation that he had twenty-four hours left to live. That was the morning he got his idea. He decided that all the exercise must have flushed out his thought processes. He called one of the guards and told him he wanted to see General Guardino. The guard had trouble understanding, since he spoke no English. Finally, when Anthony had pantomimed his way through to him, the guard grinned hugely and called an associate to share the joke. While they were still laughing, Anthony shrugged indifferently and drew his finger across his throat. Their laughter redoubled; they nodded in delight repeating the gesture and pointing at Anthony through the bars.

"*Sí. Sí,*" they said. One of them made a noose with his hands, placed it around his own neck and then jerked his head sideways, sticking out his tongue and popping his eyes. Anthony shook his head calmly, made the throat cutting gesture once more and pointed at the two guards. They stopped laughing, said something to one another, and then marched off quickly. Ten minutes later the Captain of the

183

guard was at the cell door. With him was a small, nervous civilian who worked in the police records department and who spoke a fractured sort of English.

"The Captain is wishing to knowing what you are damaging his men for?"

"Tell the Captain I want to see General Guardino." The interpreter went pale, but did as he was told. The Captain said something, which was duly translated to Anthony.

"The Captain is wishing to know what for is it that you are wishing to see the General?"

"I can't tell the Captain. Only that the General will be extremely angry if he doesn't get my message. So will the President."

There was an interchange between the Captain and the interpreter which Anthony didn't understand. Then the little man turned to him again.

"Please, you are telling the Captain something that he is telling the General, or the General not listening to the Captain and not listening to you neither, thank you."

"Have the Captain tell the General that Santos Dolivera knew where I was going to get the guns from."

This was duly translated and, while it meant very little to the Captain, he was well aware on which side his bread was buttered. He thought about it for a moment; then, without another word to Anthony, he turned and walked away. The little man started to follow him. Then he remembered his manners and turned back to Anthony. "Thanking you exceedingly," he said.

*   *   *

Guardino arrived at five in the afternoon, by which time Anthony had decided that his plan hadn't worked, and was

184

trying to remember some prayers he had learned when he was a little boy. All he could recall was something that started off with "All things bright and beautiful", and he didn't think it really fitted the occasion. There was a sudden clatter of men and rifle butts outside his cell and a moment later the door opened and Guardino strolled in. He had discarded the green fatigues favoured by his former master and was now dressed as Canstartis himself, in a neat uniform, with three gold stars on the epaulettes. He was smoking a long cheroot, the smell of which made Anthony feel slightly sick.

"I trust you are comfortable, *Señor*," he said.

"Not very."

"Never mind," said the General, "You'll not have to concern yourself much longer."

"Did you catch Dolivera yet?" asked Anthony, holding his breath for the reply.

"Not yet. But it is only a matter of time."

"I hope he comes down from the hills and cuts your balls off," said Anthony.

"That is not likely," said the General equably. "Especially as you are going to tell me what you know."

"I don't know anything."

"Yes, you do. That is why you asked to see me. You know that Dolivera has a plan."

"Me?"

"And you said that he knows where to get the arms you were going to supply to him."

"Oh, he knows *that*," said Anthony. "In fact he's probably well on his way to getting his hands on them right now."

The General smiled. "And how is he going to pay for them?"

"Credit," said Anthony. "He gets the arms on tick. As

185

soon as he is back in power he pays for them and also he gives out a contract to supply the Santhomese armed forces with all they need for the next twenty-five years."

The General became thoughtful. "He told me nothing of this."

"Of course he didn't. He was going to pay for them out of the treasury if he'd remained in power. But he mentioned it to me just in case anything happened. I told him who to contact if things went wrong."

"You realise, I suppose, that you have just confessed to a capital crime."

"So hang me."

"There's plenty of time for that,' said Guardino. "We will talk again later." He turned to go.

"Incidentally," said Anthony, who was feeling in unaccountably high spirits at this moment. "What happened to Miss Jones?"

There was a moment's pause before Guardino answered. "She is well."

"And safe?"

"For the moment."

"Meaning she might not be later on?"

Guardino shrugged, "We live in troubled times, *Señor* Bridges." And he walked out.

*   *   *

The dinner brought to him that evening was far better than he had been getting. While he was eating it the Captain came into his cell. He pointed at the food. "Okay?" he asked.

Anthony nodded. "Okay."

Obviously impressed with the way Anthony had managed

186

to conjure up a full General, the Captain produced a packet of cigarettes and held them towards Anthony.

Anthony shook his head. "No, thank you."

The Captain continued to hold them towards him, and again Anthony shook his head. The Captain started to look worried. He opened the packet, took one out, lit it and puffed away furiously for a moment. "Okay! Okay!" he said finally, having shown Anthony that the cigarette was neither poisonous nor explosive. To keep him happy, Anthony took the proffered packet and the Captain left the cell smiling.

*   *   *

At midnight, Anthony started worrying again. It was unlikely that anything would happen that night, and the following morning was going to be awfully tight for time. Perhaps he hadn't managed to get his message through to Guardino. He debated whether it was worth another try, this time asking to see *El Presidente* himself; then he decided against it. Either Guardino had told the President or he hadn't; in either case, there was nothing to do but to wait. Knowing that he wouldn't be able to sleep, he lay down on his bed anyway and started to review his life. If he was going to meet his Maker tomorrow, he wanted to make sure he presented himself with all the facts straight. But it proved to be a pretty dull exercise, and fifteen minutes later he was sound asleep.

He was still asleep at two in the morning when they came to fetch him. The Captain handed him over to another officer who escorted him to a car and they were driven to the palace. Canstartis was in the palace projection room when Anthony was ushered into his presence. The room was in darkness save for the flickering light of the screen, and Anthony bumped around for a few moments until he located a seat. After

187

a moment his eyes became accustomed to the darkness. At the same time he realised what was going on up there on the screen. It was a blue movie, one of the bluest Anthony had ever seen. It involved three girls and two men, one of whom still had his socks on. In spite of himself, Anthony found that he was fascinated with the geometric permutations that the five performers worked out, and it wasn't until three or four minutes later that he pulled himself together sufficiently to look around the projection room. As far as he could see there was only one other occupant and he was sprawled in a deep armchair placed close to the screen. Wondering if he shouldn't perhaps make his presence known, Anthony cleared his throat noisily. He was answered with an angry "Sshhh!" from the front. And because there didn't seem to be anything else to do, Anthony sat back to watch the movie. The reel ran out ten minutes later. Suddenly the lights went on and Anthony found himself blinking towards Canstartis, who had turned towards him in his armchair close to the screen.

"Whenever I have a problem," said Canstartis, without preamble, "I watch blue films. I find that they relax me. They clear the mind and I can think more profitably."

"Interesting," said Anthony.

He had taken a quick look around and realised that he had been correct in his assumption that they were the only two occupants of the room.

Now Constartis stood up, stretched and yawned prodigiously.

"I am very tired," he said. "I have not been to bed for three days. Disposing of a revolution is tiring work, as you probably realise."

"I hadn't thought about it much."

188

"Made more tiresome by your involvement, *Señor* Bridges," said Canstartis, not looking sleepy any longer.

"I'm sorry."

Canstartis brushed aside the apology, then sat down once more and punched a button on the arm of his chair. The next film started almost immediately. Canstartis indulged himself with a couple of minutes' silence; then, with his eyes still glued to the screen, he started talking again.

"Is it true?" he asked.

"What?" said Anthony, thinking he was referring to something that two girls were doing on the screen.

"Is it true that Dolivera knows where to pick up the arms that he ordered?"

"Yes."

"And that he can take possession of them without paying?"

"Yes," said Anthony again.

"You are lying, *Señor* Bridges," said Canstartis, still looking at the screen. "I have dealt with armament companies all my life. Some are honest, most are dishonest. But, honest or dishonest, there is one thing they all have in common. They all require cash on delivery."

"Ah yes," said Anthony, starting to grope. "But you are talking about private arms dealers."

"As opposed to what?"

"As opposed to governments."

There was a long pause as Canstartis digested this. "What government?" he asked finally.

"The British," said Anthony.

Canstartis stood up suddenly and turned to face Anthony. Multiple fornication was taking place across his chest where he stood in the beam from the projector. "The British?" he

189

repeated, as though it were a dirty word that he didn't quite understand.

"Yes, sir," said Anthony, wondering what he had started.

"The British?" said Canstartis again, his voice incredulous.

"Yes, sir, the British," said Anthony. Then he had a brainwave. "If you'll check you'll find out that a member of the British Embassy visited me in my cell a couple of days ago."

Canstartis brushed that aside. "That was to revoke your passport. They told us about it."

"That's what they may have told you, sir."

Canstartis stood where he was for a moment while the two girls writhed ecstatically across his chest. Then he leaned forward and punched the button by the side of his chair Immediately the film stopped and the lights came on once more.

"Follow me," he said to Anthony.

Anthony trotted after him along troop-lined corridors and into the Presidential anteroom. A sleepy aide lurched to his feet as Canstartis stalked in, hastily trying to hide a cigarette in his cupped hand. But Canstartis didn't even bother to look at him. He walked straight through into his own office with Anthony following him. There, he sat down behind his desk.

"Explain yourself, please," he said to Anthony, without asking him to sit down.

"Explain what?" said Anthony, who was still trying to work out how to enlarge on the bombshell he had just delivered.

"You said the British. Why would the British wish to arm Dolivera?"

"Policy," said Anthony.

"What policy?"

Anthony, crossing his fingers behind his back, offered up a

190

quick prayer and started talking. "It has long been felt in Her Majesty's Governmental circles that the influence of Britain as a world power has been declining."

"Ha!" said Canstartis.

"I beg your pardon?"

"Britain hasn't been a world power for fifty years. She's a little island, constantly verging on bankruptcy, supported by the countries she once ruled and which she was stupid enough to hand back to the natives."

"The Commonwealth is a powerful entity."

"The Commonwealth is a crutch for an ailing and senile grandmother."

"Be that as it may," said Anthony. "Her Majesty's Government now feel that they would like to restore some of the power and influence that made Britain great."

"In Santhoma?" said Canstartis, incredulous once more.

"First, Santhoma. Next, Peru and Chile. Finally the whole of the South American continent. Withdrawing from our responsibilities East of Suez is just a blind. While everyone in the West worries about plugging the gap we have left there, we quietly move in here."

"I don't believe you."

"You are hanging me tomorrow," said Anthony. "Why should I lie to you?"

"True," said Canstartis. 'Sit down." Anthony sat. "Why do the British wish to see Dolivera in power in Santhoma?"

"He has intimated that he would be sympathetic to the British cause. When Santhoma is made a colony, he will be created Governor General."

"Only dominions have Governor Generals."

"I mean High Commissioner," said Anthony quickly.

"Why did they not aproach me with their propositions?"

191

"Would you have agreed?"

"No."

"There is your answer."

"And what do the British think the Americans are going to do when they see a colonial power trying to move into South America?"

"The Americans can do nothing; they are the biggest colonial power of them all."

"True," said Canstartis. "And what is your part in all this, *Señor* Bridges?"

"I am just a civil servant," said Anthony. "I do what my Government tells me to."

There was a long pause during which Canstartis started to doodle with a paper knife, gouging pieces out of the leather that topped his desk. "Are you well paid?" he asked finally.

"Not very," said Anthony. "But there is a pension at sixty."

"Here in Santhoma we pay our civil servants extremely well. And there is a pension at fifty; earlier if you choose."

"I see."

"Perhaps something mutually advantageous can be arranged," said Canstartis, after another slight pause.

"Advantageous to whom?"

"To yourself and to Santhoma."

"Perhaps."

"I will be frank with you, *Señor* Bridges. I have no wish to see Santhoma become a British colony. I do not like the British. Nothing personal you understand; I do not like the Americans, the Russians or the Chinese either, but I think I like the British least of all."

"Really," said Anthony. "Why is that?"

"They are pompous, self-opinionated, hypocritical, and very stuffy." He was completely right, thought Anthony, so

192

he said nothing. After a moment Canstartis continued, "Therefore I think we will do two things. First you will tell me where and when Dolivera is picking up the arms; second you will write down everything you have told me and I shall present it to the United Nations."

"I didn't know Santhoma was a member."

"We're not. But we shall join. Then we will see how long Britain is prepared to go on playing this underhanded game."

"I'm afraid I won't be able to help you," said Anthony.

"Of course you will. I shall extract your fingernails and pour boiling oil up your anus until you do," said Canstartis equably.

"You misunderstand me," said Anthony. "When I say I won't help you, it is because I can't. I am unable to."

"You told Guardino you knew where the arms were going to be picked up."

"No, sir. I told him that Dolivera knew. I just gave Dolivera the contact to make; the contact was going to arrange delivery."

"Then we will prevent the contact."

"We can't. It's been made . . . three days ago."

"Oh," said Canstartis. He gouged another chunk of leather from the desk top. "We will deal with that aspect later then," he said. "We will now draft the letter to the United Nations."

"I can't do that either, sir."

"Why not?"

"Well, I *can* do it, but it won't do any good. Britain will just deny what I say; as proof they will show that they have taken away my passport. They will say I am an undesirable adventurer who is lying simply to save his own skin."

"True," said Canstartis. "In which case there is only one course open to us."

"Yes, sir?"

"We will prepare to meet Dolivera with force. You will go to the British and tell them that their puppet is going to have to fight a full scale war if they hope to achieve the results they're after. And still they are not going to achieve them, because it is a war that neither Dolivera nor the British can hope to win."

"Why not?"

"Have you met many Santhomese, *Señor* Bridges?"

"No, sir. Only yourself, Dolivera and some of your officers."

"If you had, you would understand better. The Santhomese are a pig-headed, aggressive, unimaginative people. They hate everyone and everything with complete impartiality. But there is one thing that they hate more than anything else; an outsider meddling in what they consider their own affair. I shall go on the radio and tell them that Dolivera is a traitor to their country and is opening the door to British rule. That way he will not even have an army because all his troops will desert him."

"I thought they already had. They're all fighting for you now."

Canstartis shrugged. "That is for today, and even perhaps for next week. But given any encouragement at all, they would be happy to desert back again to the other side. After all, they did it for me. But when I tell them that Dolivera is working for an outside power, then they will not desert. It is as simple as that."

"Dolivera can use mercenaries."

"Then my army will repel them."

"With what?"

"Ah," said Canstartis, as though he had just received

some great revelation. "You are right, of course. Where's that list again?" He searched through some papers on his desk and finally came up with a copy of the list that Dolivera had given to Anthony. He read through it quickly. "What does he want with a frigate I wonder," he said finally.

"He said he needed it to protect his coastal waters."

"Against what?"

"He didn't say."

"He was probably going to convert it into a private yacht, a floating gin palace and brothel."

"Probably," said Anthony.

"This is an impressive list," said Canstartis, after glancing through it again.

"Forty million dollars."

"That much? Still, he's not going to pay for it, is he? He's creating a national debt before he comes to power."

"You could say that."

Canstartis looked at the list a moment longer, then placed it flat on the desk and slammed the palm of his hand down on to it with a report like a pistol shot. "Very well," he said. "I shall take twenty-five per cent more."

"Twenty-five per cent more what?"

"Everything. He has ordered ten thousand rifles. I will take twelve and a half thousand. Two hundred machine guns; I will take two hundred and fifty. We'll forget the frigate, I already have a yacht at Nice."

"You can't forget the frigate, sir. Dolivera will have one," Anthony pointed out.

"Quite right," said Canstartis. "Then I shall take two frigates."

"May I suggest motor torpedo boats? You should be able

to get half a dozen for the price of a frigate. They're much faster. And after it's all over you'll be able to sell them to the rich Santhomese for conversion."

"There aren't any rich Santhomese," said Canstartis. "But I'll take the motor torpedo boats anyway."

"Six?"

"Four."

"Six would be better."

"I'll take five," said Canstartis in a tone that brooked no more argument. Then he became thoughtful suddenly. "Where are you going to get all these things from?" he asked.

"The Americans," said Anthony, albeit doubtfully.

"Why should the Americans sell me guns? I've asked them before and they've always refused. Coca-cola they will sell me; guns never."

"I'll tell them about Dolivera's order."

"That won't do any good. They'll simply go to the British Government and wave their big stick at them."

"Not if I tell them that Dolivera is buying from the Russians."

Canstartis grinned suddenly. "I like that, *Señor* Bridges. I like that very much. Perhaps if you are persuasive enough they will *give* us what we ask for."

"I doubt that," said Anthony.

Canstartis shrugged. "Perhaps you are right. But fifty million dollars is a great deal of money to find."

"Look at it this way, sir," said Anthony, warming to the subject. "After you defeat Dolivera you can confiscate the arms that he has bought. Then you can blackmail the British into buying them back for forty million. That way you will only have spent ten million."

196

"The British won't buy back arms they've never been paid for. Apart from anything else, they won't be able to afford it."

"They can borrow the money from the Americans. The Americans will lend it because they have just been paid fifty million dollars by you; it'll be surplus money."

"But they have sold me arms for that fifty million."

"You can give them the arms back. After all, with Dolivera defeated, you won't need them; not for some little time anyway."

Canstartis was silent for a long time as he and Anthony tried to work out the logistics of what they had both been discussing. There had to be a snag somewhere, thought Anthony, but for the life of him he couldn't spot it. He thought about it for a long time, then he started to work the whole thing out backwards; he was halfway through this exercise when he realised that he was wasting his time. The whole story had been built up to get him off a hanging, and there wasn't a word of truth in it. Dolivera didn't know where to get the arms because Anthony hadn't contacted Walpole; and even if he had, it certainly wasn't going to be from the British. Anthony sat back and breathed a sigh of relief; he had been so engrossed in his plotting that he had quite forgotten that the whole thing was a work of fiction and, if he had managed to fool himself, he should have been able to fool Canstartis. He glanced across at the President. Canstartis was tilted back in his chair gazing hard at the ceiling. At one moment it looked as though he were going to ask a question, then he changed his mind and shifted his gaze to the far wall. After five minutes he got up and paced a little, then he sat down again. He made a couple of quick notes on a piece of scrap paper, looked at them, then tore them up. Finally he sat back and looked at Anthony.

"Agreed," he said.

*   *   *

They had a drink to celebrate. Then they had another. Finally it was five in the morning and Anthony felt marvellous. Feeling that he had reached the state where he could ask the President for a favour or two, he approached the first of his requests.

"I would appreciate seeing Miss Jones again," he said.

"Who?"

"Miss Jones. The lady who was with me when I was arrested."

"Ah," said Canstartis.

"I don't quite get your meaning."

Canstartis wandered over and poured himself another drink. "That may prove a little difficult," he said finally.

"Oh?" said Anthony. "Why is that?"

"You are in love with her, are you not."

"How did you know?"

Canstartis came back over to his desk and pulled a sheet of paper from among some others. Anthony recognised it as the letter he had written to Shirleen from his cell. "Because you say so in this letter."

There didn't seem much point in complaining about invasion of privacy, so he didn't bother. Instead he tried to find out what had happened to Shirleen.

"She is safe," said Canstartis.

"So why can't I see her?"

"She is a hostage. Hostages we keep incommunicado."

"Hostage for what?"

198

"For you, of course, *Señor* Bridges. If you carry out every term of our agreement, she will be released to your care. No doubt her gratitude will be unbounded."

"What if something goes wrong?"

"I shall have her killed."

That's torn it, thought Anthony.

8

AT TEN O'CLOCK THE FOLLOWING DAY, ANTHONY
was handed a new passport. He had been made a citizen of
Santhoma overnight, and the red covered passport attested to
the fact. The passport also stated that Anthony was to be
granted diplomatic privileges wherever he went which, he
thought, was a splendid idea. As he was being driven to the
airport in the President's own car, he made one last attempt
to try to see Shirleen.

"At least let me see her to tell her that everything is going
to be all right."

"I will tell her," said Guardino, who was in the car with
him.

200

"She'd take it better from me."

"No doubt. But she will have to be satisfied with hearing it from me."

"How do I know she's still alive?"

"You don't," said Guardino equably, and that seemed to close the conversation.

*   *   *

The drive to the airport was uneventful if one discounted the trouble they had getting through the main square. Anthony's coming hanging had been well advertised and half of Santhoma seemed to have come into town for the event. Even the presence of a dozen motor-cyclist outriders escorting the car wasn't too successful in clearing a path through the crowds. Then somebody recognised Anthony from a photograph that had appeared at the time of the trial and, thinking he was being driven to the gallows, a path cleared miraculously. As they drove past the gallows and continued on out of the main square, they could hear a great yell of rage and frustration from the crowd they had left behind. "They're going to be very disappointed," said Anthony.

"No, they won't," said Guardino. "We're hanging someone else."

"Who?"

"It's not important."

"Not to you perhaps."

"Nor to him. He was going to be shot."

*   *   *

Just before they reached the airport, Guardino, who had remained quiet during most of the journey, leaned forward and checked that the partition separating them from the

201

guard and the driver was fully closed. Then he sat back once more and, when he started talking, it was quietly.

"*El Presidente* has told me very little of what you and he discussed last night, *Señor* Bridges."

"Really?"

"Would you care to enlighten me?"

"Not much."

"It could be advantageous."

"To whom?"

"To both of us. You see, here in Santhoma, it is always wise to invest in the future. But before one does that it is helpful to know which way the future is going to turn."

"You've managed pretty well up to now, General. You were on Dolivera's side when he took over and, now that Canstartis is back, you're still up there; and promoted with it."

"That is because I take good care to be in the right place at the right time. But it is necessary to know what is imminent from one day to the next."

"You'll just have to guess at this one, General," said Anthony. "If the President wants you to know what he's doing, he'll tell you."

"Mmm," said Guardino thoughtfully.

"One thing I can tell you, though."

"Yes?" said Guardino attentively.

"Don't order any new uniforms." And he boarded the aircraft ten minutes later happy in the knowledge that he had left a worried man behind him.

*   *   *

As the plane took off, heading North, the only cloud on Anthony's horizon was Shirleen. Where was she now? And

202

was she all right? He tried to visualise her lovely young body, languishing in some dirty, fly blown cell, but the image upset him so much that he turned it off quickly. Still, he was going to win her freedom; and hadn't Canstartis said that her gratitude would be unbounded? Relaxing a little with visions of Shirleen's unbounded gratitude, he dozed off and didn't awaken until the stewardess shook him gently to tell him that the aircraft had just touched down in Andestina.

*   *   *

The hotel was depressing without Shirleen, each face and room recalling something of the marvellous time they had spent there together. The overall impact was such that Anthony nearly checked out after the first couple of hours. But there didn't seem to be another decent place in the city and there were a couple of dolly birds from the French Embassy disporting themselves by the side of the pool, so he decided to clear his mind of misery and anguish, and get on with what he had come here for. Three hours after checking in, his telephone call to London came through.

"What do you want?" It was Walpole's Miss Cremin of the saltbeef sandwiches and grotty disposition.

"I'd like to speak to Mr. Walpole, please."

"You can't. He's out."

"Then I'd like to leave a message," said Anthony. "Have you got a pencil?"

"Of course I've got a pencil," she snapped back at him.

"I have an order for him. Ready?"

"*Do* get on with it. The kettle's boiling."

"I'd like twelve and a half thousand AR 10s. They're rifles . . ."

"I know what they are."

203

"Two hundred and fifty light machine guns. Thirty Cossack armoured cars. Twenty-five light anti-tank guns. Two hundred and fifty tons of napalm. Two hundred and fifty tons of nerve gas. And five motor torpedo boats. I've quoted a price of fifty million dollars." He paused, waiting for some sort of comment from the other end. Finally, it came. "Is that all?"

"That's all."

"Good-bye." And the line went dead.

Feeling somewhat anti-climatical, Anthony went downstairs to the pool where he started to make a play for the two girls from the French Embassy.

*   *   *

"Anthony, my dear old friend. You are supposed to be hanging from your throat." It was Carlos Ramirez. Anthony had made a date with the two girls and then come up to his room for a sleep. Now he was being shaken awake by a jubilant Carlos.

"How did you get in?" asked Anthony, bad tempered at having been wakened.

"I am bribing the chambers maid. As soon as I am learning from my spies that you are here, I am coming rapidly. Why are you not hanging by your throat?"

"Canstartis changed his mind," said Anthony, struggling out of bed.

"I am a happy, happy man," said Carlos, following Anthony into the bathroom. "I am weeping for two whole days when I am hearing that you are hanging."

"You might have tried something more practical," said Anthony. "Like helping me escape."

Carlos spread his hands wide. "What could I be doing,

204

old friend? If I am staying in Santhoma any longer they are probably hanging me, too. Instead I am coming here, where I work for your release."

"Doing what?"

Carlos shrugged. "I write letters. I talk to people. I talk to many, many people. I even go to the British Embassy for you."

"What did they say?"

"They are saying that you have your passport revoked in Santhoma and you are no longer Englishman."

"Wait till they hear what I cooked up for them with Canstartis."

"Then I am hearing that you are here and I am knowing that all my working for you has been rewarding," said Carlos.

"Thank you, Carlos," said Anthony, still full of sleep.

"Is nothing," said Carlos modestly. "And now we are getting down to business. No?"

"No," said Anthony.

Carlos looked sad suddenly. "But why not. Business you must be having or you would not be here."

"Business I am having," said Anthony. "But I am not needing you to perform it."

Carlos looked even sadder. "But you are needing me badly," he said. "You cannot perform business here without the knowledge and experiencing of Carlos Ramirez."

"Yes I can," said Anthony, who wasn't feeling at all well disposed towards Carlos. Exactly what Carlos could have accomplished back in Santhoma, he didn't know, but there must have been something. A man with Carlos' connections should have been able to get a man out of prison like shelling peas. Carlos followed him out of the bathroom.

"You are angry with Carlos?" he said.

205

"I am not angry," said Anthony. "I am just not very pleased."

"Is same thing," said Carlos. He watched Anthony for a short time while he was getting dressed, his face growing longer and longer. Finally he stood up and headed for the door. "I am saying good-bye then."

"Good-bye," said Anthony.

After a moment's hesitation Carlos turned and walked out. Anthony felt a momentary twinge of guilt, but before it had time to enlarge, the phone rang. It was Walpole calling from London.

"I thought you were being hanged," he said for openers.

"They changed their minds."

"What's this list Miss Cremin has given me?"

"It's a fifty million dollar order." There was a silence from the other end. "Hello," said Anthony. "Are you still there?"

"I'm here," said Walpole.

"When and where can I pick the stuff up?"

"You can't," said Walpole. "We don't have it."

"You can get it though?"

"No, we can't," said Walpole. "We're going out of business."

"I'm sorry," said Anthony. "The line's bad. For a moment I thought you said we were going out of business."

"I did," said Walpole. "Money due to you has been deposited in your Swiss bank. Your credit cards have been cancelled. Good-bye."

"Wait a minute," said Anthony. "You can't just go out of business like that."

"We have already done so."

"Am I allowed to know the reason?"

"I see no reason why not," said Walpole. "Except that this telephone call is costing money."

"I'll pay it," said Anthony. "Stop it out of my money."

"Very well," said Walpole. "There was a takeover in Lamboola. The new government confiscated all foreign property in the country, which included our entire arsenal."

"But nothing like that ever happens in Lamboola. Your man Carter told me so."

"Carter is now Commander-in-Chief of the army and Minister for War."

"Oh," said Anthony. "Who are they fighting?"

"Nobody at present, but I believe they have their eyes on the Union of South Africa. Lamboola is now the most powerfully armed nation *per capita* in the world."

"But you don't have to go out of business. You can get new stock."

"Mr. H. has decided that he doesn't want to be involved in the armaments business any longer. There have been some articles in *The Times* recently. It is bad for his image."

"I didn't know he had one," said Anthony, remembering Henshawe when he had seen him the first time.

"He has decided to run for Parliament as a Socialist. We are lunching at Downing Street tomorrow."

"We?"

"I am his political agent, naturally," said Walpole.

"Naturally."

"And now, if there is nothing else, I have my lunch to eat."

Anthony visualised the salt beef sandwiches and the lukewarm tea. "*Bon appétit*," he said.

"Are you being facetious?" asked Walpole from seven thousand miles away.

207

"No, sir," said Anthony. "But I must get that order filled. Someone's life depends on it."

Walpole chuckled; it was the first time Anthony had heard him make such a sound. "With an order like this I should imagine a great many lives depended on it. Good-bye." And the line went dead.

*　　*　　*

Anthony went to find Carlos. There had to be other places where he could obtain what Canstartis needed, and if anyone would know where, it would be Carlos. He asked at the reception desk.

"No, *Señor. Señor* Ramirez is not staying in the hotel. No, *señor,* we have no idea where he might be located."

So he went outside to see if the doorman had heard Carlos say anything to a cab driver or chauffeur.

"No, *señor.* But why not ask that taxi driver over there. He has been hanging around for two hours now."

Anthony walked over to the taxi and stuck his head in the driver's window. "Excuse me," he said. "Do you speak English?"

The taxi driver grinned, exposing a mouthful of steel teeth.

"*Sí, señor,* I speak English very good. You will get into my taxi cab, please." As though to lend some weight to his invitation, he produced a large gun from somewhere and stuck it practically up Anthony's nose. Somewhat confused, Anthony started to withdraw his head. At the same time he became conscious of two men who had moved up behind him.

"Do like he says," said one of the men, with a heavy American accent.

"Or you'll bleed all over the pavement," said the other.

The driver reached back and opened the rear door. One

208

of the men got in first, then Anthony, then the other man. It wasn't until the car had started up, pulling into the traffic, that Anthony took a look at his new companions.

"Don't I know you?" he asked the tall thin one with the outsized adam's apple.

"Harvey Dacron," said the man. Anthony looked at the other one.

"Stanley Parsons," said the short man.

"We met right here in the hotel a couple of weeks ago," said Anthony, remembering the encounter.

"Right," said Dacron. "When you lied to us."

"About the Ambassador," said Parsons.

"I did no such thing," said Anthony, indignantly.

"He's been recalled," said Dacron.

"To Washington," said Parsons.

Anthony thought about this for a couple of minutes and suddenly had a bright idea. "Oh, I see now. You thought I was referring to the American Ambassador."

"Weren't you?" said Dacron.

"Of course not. I don't even know the American Ambassador. I was talking about *Señor* Alvira, the Ambassador from Santhoma."

The two Americans flashed one another a glance, but neither said anything.

"So now that you know it was just a simple misunderstanding perhaps you'll drive me back to the hotel. I have rather a lot to do."

"Can't do that," said Parsons.

"Orders," said Dacron.

"Whose orders?"

"Ours."

"But who are you?" asked Anthony.

"Peace Corps," said Dacron.

"So shut up or we'll mutilate you a bit," said Parsons.

Anthony shut up and spent the remainder of the journey wondering why the Peace Corps should be coming after him with guns.

*   *   *

"We don't like what you are doing. Mr. Bridges," said the Ambassador. "No, sir, we don't like it one little bit." He was a large man, about sixty years old, with a craggy, mid-Western type face and snow-white hair cut short. He gave an immediate impression of strength and integrity which lasted until one moved close to him. Then his glass eye became obvious. It was the left one, and it remained motionless in its socket while its companion wandered about like all eyes are supposed to. Added to this, the glass eye didn't quite match the good one for colour. Once one noticed this physical defect the Ambassador wasn't nearly as prepossessing an individual.

"What don't you like, sir?" asked Anthony politely. Dacron and Parsons were hovering about somewhere behind him and he didn't want to appear to be stroppy.

"Dealing in arms, sir; that's what we don't like. Dealing in instruments of death and destruction. No, sir, we don't like it one little bit. And by 'we', I refer of course to the Government of the United States of America."

"Of course," said Anthony.

"We in the United States of America are a peace loving people. Peace is our natural and our national heritage; some of our greatest leaders have been assassinated in their fight for peace; we are engaged in a major war for peace. Billions of dollars are spent annually on armaments. What for? For

210

peace. Peace, sir, non-violence, pacifism, brotherly love; these are our tenets. And by God, sir, we'll kill anyone who doesn't go along with them. Do you understand me, sir?"

"Yes, sir," said Anthony.

"I'm glad to hear it. Now we've got nothing against you personally. You're just a young fella trying to make an honest buck. We admire that in the United States of America. Next to peace, we hold that it's every man's God-given right to earn a living doing exactly what he chooses. Right?"

"Right."

"But in your case, you've got to start doing something else, son, because if you don't, then, sure as God made little green apples, you're going to wake up in some dark alley with your head split wide open. Understand?"

"No, sir."

"Good," said the Ambassador. Then it registered. "What do you mean, 'no sir'?"

"I'm sure that everything you have been saying is extremely pertinent to your fellow countrymen. But I am not an American. I'm British ... er ... that is Santhomese. And now, if you'll excuse me, I've got to go out and buy fifty million dollars' worth of assorted death."

The Ambassador had frozen rigid as he listened to Anthony. His good eye had gone so dead that there seemed to be more life in the glass one. There was a long silence as Anthony finished, broken finally by the Ambassador.

"You're in serious trouble, son," he said.

"Tell me about it."

"I will," said the Ambassador. "I sure as hell will. If there's one thing we can't stand it's your kind of pink, bigoted, pseudo-intellectual, left-wing radicalism. Yes, sir, you're in a great deal of trouble. Bad, bad trouble."

"You already said that, sir," said Anthony.

"And I meant it, son. I really did mean it."

"You were going to tell me about it."

"All in good time," said the Ambassador. Then he nodded his head slowly. "Yes, sirree; big, big trouble." This was followed by a long silence, during which Anthony sat down again.

The Ambassador continued to nod his head a few more times. "Big, big trouble," he said finally.

"May I go now?" asked Anthony.

The Ambassador looked up. "Mm? Oh yes; get along, son. Take care."

Anthony turned towards the door which was opened for him by Dacron. He and Parsons followed Anthony out of the Ambassador's office.

"We were better off with the last one," said Parsons.

"And he was a stupid prick," said Dacron.

"Let's go get a drink," said Parsons.

"Fine by me," said Dacron. They both looked towards Anthony. "Drink?"

"Why not," said Anthony.

*   *   *

There was a bar next door to the Embassy, a quiet, cosy bar, air conditioned and underlit. Dacron and Parsons escorted Anthony into the place and were greeted by the bartender-cum-manager as though they were the owners.

Anthony remarked on this. Parsons laughed.

"We *are* the owners," said Dacron.

"A sideline," said Parsons.

Anthony noticed that all the booze and cigarettes on sale in the place were American, and all carried the seal of the

American PX. He agreed with his two companions that he would join them in a large scotch and water, then sat back while they tried to work out a scheme to have the incumbent Ambassador recalled.

"We could get some of the local lads to throw rocks at the Embassy," said Dacron. "Then tell him the Commies are responsible."

"We could kidnap his old lady. Blame that on the Reds as well."

"He'd call out the Embassy heavy squad . . ."

"That's us."

". . . and we'll pop off a couple of local natives."

"Then tell Washington it's what he told us to do."

"And that should wrap it up."

They drank to this, told Anthony to finish his drink, and called for another round. During the next drink they worked out how they were going to arrange the abduction of the Ambassador's wife; the third drink covered the organisation of the anti-American riot they were going to mount; the fourth drink took care of the couple of natives they were going to pop off; the fifth drink provided a résumé of the entire scheme; then they ordered a sixth to toast their plan. Ten minutes later they called up the seventh drink.

"Wha's your problem ol' buddy?" said Dacron to Anthony who was quietly crying into his seventh scotch on the rocks.

"S'my girl."

"Never mind," said Parsons, with a sympathetic catch in his voice. "All right. Always ish."

"Tell you what you do," said Dacron. "Go call her up. Tell her you forgive her."

"Can't do that," sobbed Anthony. "She's in prison."

"Let's spring her,' said Dacron, sitting up to attention and pulling a large gun from beneath his jacket.

"Good idea," said Parsons, also producing a gun. "Into battle!" They both tried to get to their feet and failed miserably. "We'll spring her tomorrow," said Dacron.

"We're kidnapping the Ambassador's wife tomorrow," said Parsons.

"The old cow will have to wait. First we spring our ol' buddy's broad out of the pokey. Which pokey's she in, ol' buddy?"

"I don' know," said Anthony, starting to cry again; he was deeply touched by the concern of his new-found friends.

"Wha's she in for?" said Dacron. "Hooking?"

Anthony shook his head again. "Don' know what she's in for. Yes I do. Accsheshory to gun-running."

"A female gun-runner. Haven't come across one of them before."

"She's not a gun-runner," said Anthony. "She's a beautiful innocent young creature trapped by circumstances over which she had no control."

"My God, tha's beautiful!" said Dacron with feeling.

"Tha's the most beautiful thing I ever heard," said Parsons.

"Let's drink to our ol' buddy buddy and his mother."

"She's not my mother."

"Whassamatter with you. You got a mother, ain't you?" Anthony nodded, too choked up to speak. "So le's drink to her." The drinks were ordered, but by the time they arrived Dacron and Parsons had forgotten what the toast was to be, and Anthony had never really worked it out in the first place. He downed his drink and lurched to his feet.

"Got to go shopping," he said.

"We'll come with you," said Parsons.

"What you shopping for?" asked Dacron.

"Guns, napalm, armoured cars; stuff like that," said Anthony, groping in his pocket for his shopping list.

"Hey," said Dacron. "Sounds like fun."

"Lesh go," said Parsons.

*　　*　　*

The three of them staggered out into the street and stood for a moment, blinded by the sunlight.

"Where's the armoured car shop?" asked Dacron.

"I want to buy the napalm first," said Parsons.

"All right," said Dacron. "Where's the napalm shop?"

They both looked towards Anthony.

"I don't know," said Anthony.

"Lesh go back inside," said Dacron. "This daylights giving me double vision."

They went back into the bar and ordered another drink. While they were drinking it, Anthony managed to locate his shopping list. He showed it to them and told them how he needed to get the stuff for Canstartis or he'd never see his beloved Shirleen again. Both men were in tears by the time he had finished.

"Wha' we goin' to do for our ol' buddy?" said Parsons.

"We're goin' to help him, tha's what," said Dacron. He called for the telephone and when it arrived and was plugged in, he started to dial a number. Halfway through, he stopped. "Whassa number of the Embashy?" he asked.

"Whose Embashy?"

"The Embashy of the United States of America."

"Tha's our Embashy."

"Right. Whassa number?"

Parsons thought about it for a few moments, then he shook

215

his head. "Forgotten. I know the Russian Embashy."

"That'll do," said Dacron.

After some difficulty he managed to dial the Russian Embassy. "Gregor Invanovitch," he said into the phone. A moment later he was connected.

"Gregor. This is Harvey Dacron. How are you Greg ol' buddy buddy? Tha's good; glad to hear it. How's Olga and the kids? I love those kids. Hey look, Gregor, wha's all this about your lot selling guns to the rebels in Santhoma?"

9

ANTHONY HAD NEVER BEEN TO AMERICA. SOME time ago he had decided that it was going to be one of those places he was just never going to see. He would have preferred to be flying to New York or San Francisco, but even so, the thought of Los Angeles was quite exciting. Dacron and Parsons had seen him off at the airport; they had adopted Anthony for reasons known only to themselves, and they had steered him through the two days subsequent to their binge, telling him what to say and what not to say. Not that he had to say much; not that he could!

Immediately after Dacron's telephone call from the bar, Anthony had passed out. When he came to, he found himself back in his hotel room with the two girls from the French Embassy at his bedside, competing for the privilege of putting cold compresses on him. He had promptly passed out again. Finally, just before the top of his head split wide open, he staggered out of bed and dashed for the bathroom. As soon as he was able, he lurched into the shower cubicle, closed the door and turned on the cold water. Then he quietly slid down the wall until he was in a sitting position on the floor of the shower. Twenty minutes later he was still there and in imminent danger of drowning; his backside was jammed over the water outlet, and the level of the water in the cubicle had risen to his neck. He had also dozed off. Fortunately the girls had suddenly invaded the bathroom. They pulled open the door to the cubicle and dragged Anthony out, the released water flooding the bathroom and half the bedroom as well. It seemed he was wanted on the telephone and, as he staggered back into the bedroom, he glanced at the time. It was two o'clock in the morning.

"You're in big trouble, boy," said the voice of the American Ambassador over the phone.

"I don't need you to tell me that."

"I want you to get yourself over here right away," said the Ambassador.

"Tomorrow."

"You want that I should send my two men over there and break your arm a little?" enquired the Ambassador.

"I'll bet you can't even find them," said Anthony.

There was a pause from the other end of the line. "Do me a favour, son," said the Ambassador, pleading now.

"Why should I?"

"I've been good to you in the past."

"You only met me this afternoon."

218

"I was good to you though."

"You weren't. But I'll come over anyway," said Anthony. "On one condition."

"What's that?"

"You don't tell me I'm in big trouble again."

"Agreed," said the Ambassador, relief in his voice. "I'll send a car for you."

*   *   *

The Embassy had been humming when Anthony arrived. Worried looking men were running backwards and forwards, and the place was a blaze of light. Dacron and Parsons were nowhere in evidence and, if they felt anything like Anthony did, he didn't wonder. He had been shown straight to the Ambassador's office. The Ambassador was wearing a flamboyantly patterned silk dressing-gown over a pair of flannelette pyjamas; he had obviously mislaid his bedroom slippers because he was wearing a pair of thick-soled, sensible American type shoes. He had no socks on, and he hadn't tied the laces, which were long and flapped around his ankles, threatening to trip him up with each step that he took. But this was the least of his problems. The Ambassador looked a very worried man. "Come in, son, come in!" he said as soon as he saw Anthony. "We've got problems."

Anthony was feeling foul; apart from a grinding headache, he felt he was about to throw up at any moment. "I know what my problems are," he said. "What are yours?"

"It's those fucking Reds again," said the Ambassador. "They're shipping arms into Santhoma."

"How do you know?" asked Anthony, suddenly interested

"We intercepted a message. They're sneaky as hell these Commies. You know something, they didn't even let their

219

Embassy over here know about it. We intercepted a message from the Embassy here direct to Moscow; they wanted to know all about it. See. Moscow hadn't even told them."

"What did Moscow reply?"

"They denied it, of course. They just said they weren't shipping arms, never had, and had no intention of."

"I'm sorry," said Anthony. "I thought you said they *were* shipping arms."

" 'Course they are, son. You're not a diplomat, so it may be a little tricky for you to understand. But when they say they're *not* shipping arms, it's a damn sure thing that they *are*. Like I said, sneaky as hell."

"What would they say if they weren't shipping arms then?"

"Like as not they'd say they were. Then perhaps they wouldn't. Never can tell."

Anthony's headache had begun to feel worse. He wanted to go home. "Why are you telling me all this, sir?" he asked. "I'm not even an American, let alone a diplomat."

"I'm telling you, son, because you're heavily involved."

"I am?"

"You've got yourself a pipeline into Santhoma. Right?"

"It's hardly that."

"That's not what I heard."

"What did you hear?"

"You're the official, accredited supplier of arms to the Santhomes Government."

"Where did you hear that?"

The Ambassador nodded his head sagely. "I have my sources."

Obviously Dacron, or Parsons, hadn't passed out quite as quickly as Anthony. He tried to make some sense of what was happening, but his headache was threatening to split his

220

skull wide open any moment now. "May I go home, please," he asked.

"Home? What are you talking about? You're going to the United States of America, son."

"I'd rather go home, thank you," Anthony said. Then he had turned round and tottered out of the Embassy, making it back to the hotel just in time to pass out for the third time.

*   *   *

When he awakened just after noon the following day, the French girls had gone and his phone was ringing. It was Harvey Dacron.

"Better get your ass over to the Embassy fast, old buddy," he said.

"What's going on, Harvey?" asked Anthony. "Did I see the Ambassador last night, or did I dream it?"

"You saw him. And he's been chewing nails waiting for you to surface ever since."

"What does he want me for?"

"You've got to go to the States and pick yourself out fifty million dollars' worth of assorted mayhem to ship back to Santhoma. That way you get your girl-friend out of hock and make yourself a couple of bucks at the same time. Everyone is happy, including me and Stanley."

"What do you get out of it?"

"One: the Ambassador gets recalled because he's cocked up the *status quo* out here. Two: we get the contract to ship the stuff from Stateside to Santhoma."

"You get the shipping contract?"

"Sure. Last night me and Stanley went out and bought ourselves a ship. A sort of sideline. Three: you give us twenty-

221

five per cent of your commission on the deal. And four: we'll get a commission from the Reds, too, via my buddy Gregory."

"Commission on what?"

"On the arms they'll be shipping."

"But they're not shipping any, Harvey. They never were."

"They are now, old buddy. They heard the Americans were going to, so they're doing likewise. I tell you, the ball is rolling fast, old buddy, so just move your ass over here before it starts to slow down."

So Anthony had moved his ass over to the Embassy, and the following morning he had boarded an Air Force plane bound for Los Angeles. The Ambassador was on the aircraft with him, complete with wife, two dachshunds and all their baggage.

"I've been recalled, son," he said to Anthony. Then he moved to the rear of the aircraft and Anthony didn't see him again.

The aircraft put down at a military field near Long Beach, and there was someone waiting to meet Anthony as he stepped down from the plane.

"Buzz Handiman," he bellowed at Anthony by way of an introduction. He was six feet five inches tall and looked like solid muscle through and through. His eyes were bright blue, and his hair, which was crewcut, was very fair; his face was tanned dark brown. He was wearing the uniform of a major in the American marines, and he was quite the most formidable looking man Anthony had ever encountered.

"I'm to look after you," he said. "The Pentagon called. Said any damn thing you want. I'm to see that you get it double bloody quick."

"Very good of them," said Anthony.

222

"So what do you want?"

"I'd like a bath," said Anthony. "If that would be all right."

Handiman looked at him as though only cissies bathed, but he nodded nevertheless. "I've reserved a bungalow for you at the Beverly Hills Hotel," he said. "I'll drop you over there and come round and pick you up at seven."

"What happens at seven?"

"You wanna see the town, or don't you?"

"I'd like to very much," said Anthony.

"Fine," said Handiman. "Then tomorrow we'll fly down to New Mexico where you can sort out the stuff you want. Okay?"

"Okay," said Anthony.

*   *   *

Buzz Handiman arrived at the hotel at seven o'clock on the dot. He had changed into civilian clothes, which somehow made him look even larger, and he was carrying a brown paper bag under his arm. This he opened as soon as Anthony let him in, to disclose a bottle of Bourbon.

"Always like to pour a little oil on the bearings before starting up the motor," he said as he twisted the top off the bottle and poured himself a tumblerful of neat spirit. "Here's looking at you," he said, swallowing the drink without batting an eyelid and pouring himself another almost before Anthony had closed the door. By the time they left the hotel twenty minutes later, he had all but finished the bottle, without any effect on him whatsoever that Anthony could see.

"Where do you wanna go?" he asked as they both piled into a Cadillac convertible.

"It's my first time here," said Anthony. "I leave it up to you."

"I mean like what's your fancy? Are you a faggot?"

"No."

"You wanna see some tits?"

"Not particularly."

"You wanna crawl round some bars?"

Anthony hadn't had a drink since his afternoon bender with Dacron and Parsons. Since then, everything had happened so fast, leaving him so confused, that the thought of tying one on seemed quite attractive. "Let's do that," he said.

So they started crawling round some bars. Early in the evening it was some of the better places, Sneaky Pete's, the Cock 'n Bull and a couple of the hotel bars. Then they drifted down to Santa Monica Boulevard to Barney's Beanery and the Raincheck, and after that it was downhill all the way. About midnight they were in a bar called Hank's Place. Anthony, feeling very much under the influence, came back from the toilet to find Buzz in heated argument with two men sitting next to him at the bar.

"And I'm telling you that if you're not a white Anglo-Saxon Protestant, you're nuthin', just plain nuthin'." The men he was talking to were both as black as the ace of spades, and the remainder of the clientele in the bar were obviously of Mexican descent.

"You're full of shit," said one of the black men, and he turned his back on Buzz. What followed next was like something out of a bad Western movie. The black man who had spoken found himself on the opposite side of the bar picking broken glass out of his hair, while his companion sat on the floor complaining that Buzz had broken his leg. The bartender was on the phone to the police while the other customers sat in frozen silence, wondering whether there were any odds in pulling the knives they all obviously carried.

224

"Let's split," said Buzz, when he saw Anthony, who was trying to look as though he were on his own. So they had split and gone down the street a couple of hundred yards. To the best of Anthony's knowledge, Buzz had downed a bottle and a half of Bourbon, but he still looked as sober as a hanging judge and twice as dangerous. This bar was called just Pete's, and the entire clientele looked stoned out of their minds; there was an unmistakable smell of pot as they came in, so strong that Anthony reckoned he could get high by just breathing. Buzz moved to the bar and elbowed somebody off a stool; the displaced man was too far gone to complain. It was doubtful if he was even aware that he had been dislodged.

"Bourbon for me, scotch for the limey," bellowed Buzz at the bartender.

The bartender who was large and mean looking was at the far end of the bar talking to one of his customers. He glanced up towards Buzz, then turned back and continued his conversation. Buzz let a full second drift by before slamming his fist down on the bar so hard that every bottle in the place rattled. "Hey!" he yelled at the bartender. "Wassa matter? You got cloth ears?"

The bartender finished what he was saying and turned to look towards Buzz once more. "You speaking to me?" he asked.

"Damn right I am," said Buzz. "Now get your ass up here before I come over there and kick it up through the top of your skull."

The bartender straightened up. He was even larger than Anthony had first thought. He ambled down the bar and stopped opposite Buzz. Then he leaned forward so that their faces were inches apart.

225

"Go fuck yourself," he said, distinctly.

"What did you say!" bellowed Buzz.

"You heard me," said the bartender.

Anthony had worked out Buzz's philosophy by now; it was to hit first and argue about whether to fight or not later. He edged himself off his stool and tried to put a little distance between himself and what he knew would follow. Buzz grabbed the front of the bartender's shirt with one fist, and drew back the other preparatory to breaking the man's head open. But the bartender had seen it all before. One of his hands emerged from beneath the bar clenched round a bottle of vodka. Before Buzz could hit him, the bartender had broken the bottle over his head.

Peering at the bartender through the blood and vodka which were dripping down his face, Buzz looked surprised and strangely hurt. "What did you wanna go and do that for?" he asked.

" 'Cos you was goin' to bust me."

"Damn right," said Buzz, and busted him.

*   *   *

Two minutes later the police were all over the place and fifteen minutes after that Anthony and Buzz were in a cell. Anthony watched, disinterested, while a police doctor put half a dozen stitches into Buzz's scalp

"That'll take care of it," said the doctor, putting away his things.

"Thanks doc," said Buzz. "On your way out tell the man in charge I'd like a word with him."

"I'll tell him," said the doctor. "But I don't know whether it'll do any good."

"Tell him if he likes his job he'd better get down here."

226

Five minutes later a disgruntled police lieutenant came down to the cells.

"Whaddya want?"

"We want out," said Buzz.

"Big deal!"

"Call this number," said Buzz, handing the lieutenant a slip of paper through the bars. The lieutenant looked at it, then up at Buzz.

"What are you? Some kind of a nut? This is out of town."

"So call collect. But call, buddy, or you'll be back on the beat."

Fifteen minutes later the lieutenant was back yelling for the cell to be unlocked. He ushered Buzz and Anthony out like they were royalty.

"Sorry, fellas," he said. "No harm done I hope?"

"Nope," said Buzz, and walked out without another word. Anthony hurried after him.

"Where to now?" asked Buzz, standing by the car which the police had brought in.

"Back to the hotel?" suggested Anthony.

"You said you wanted to go out on the town."

"I thought we already had."

Buzz glanced at his watch. "Hell, it's only just past two-thirty."

"I'm tired," said Anthony, feeling it was about time for him to stick up for himself.

"Okay," said Buzz. "You're calling the shots."

They drove back to the hotel in silence. Just before they arrived Anthony asked him something. "Who did you get the lieutenant to telephone?"

"Washington," said Buzz, without taking his eyes off the road.

"You must carry quite a bit of weight," said Anthony, impressed.

"Not me, friend," said Buzz. "But you do." He pulled up outside the hotel, and leaning across, opened the door. "Pick you up at seven-thirty," he said.

"I thought we were going to New Mexico tomorrow," said Anthony.

"We are."

"Shouldn't we start a little earlier then?"

"If you like," said Buzz indifferently. "Make it seven."

It wasn't until Buzz drove off that Anthony realised that he had been referring to a.m., not p.m.

*   *   *

It was gone three o'clock before Anthony climbed into bed. He arranged for the hotel to call him at six-thirty; then he settled down for his three and a half hours of sleep. But it wouldn't come. A mish-mash of impressions paraded before him, and he decided after fifteen minutes that he had never felt so wide awake in his life. He got out of bed again and went into the kitchen to see if the hotel had put anything in his refrigerator. They hadn't, so he wandered around the bungalow trying to work up a tiredness. What was it that Buzz Handiman had said? Anthony carried weight in Washington. He wondered why, and whether that weight could be used to restore his British passport. He could ask Washington to lean on London a little; threaten to recall an international loan or somesuch; that should do the trick. He mused on this for ten minutes or so, then decided to have another shot at sleep. He tossed and turned, and then started to think of Shirleen, which only made him toss and turn some more.

228

Then, about six a.m., he finally drifted off to sleep; at six-thirty he was really deep when the phone rang with his wake-up call.

*   *   *

Buzz was wearing his uniform again this morning. He stood in the hotel lobby impatiently, looking at his watch as Anthony came down.

"You're late," he said. It was three minutes past seven.

"I'm sorry," said Anthony. "Good morning."

Buzz grunted something in reply and they walked out to the waiting car. Anthony felt like seventeen different kinds of death, all painful; added to this he had received a major shock fifteen minutes ago when he had looked at himself in the bathroom mirror. His eyes looked like an Arizona sunset, and they were supported on pouches as large and shapeless as badly packed duffle bags. Whereas Buzz Handiman looked as though he had just returned from a month spent at a health clinic; he was clean shaven, which Anthony wasn't, and he glowed with good health and vitality. His step was springy and his carriage erect. Anthony decided that he had never met anyone he disliked quite so much. He slouched next to Buzz in the rear of the car, while the Marine driver took them back out to the Long Beach military airfield. The only blessing of the morning was that Buzz didn't seem inclined to talk, which suited Anthony fine. At the airfield they transferred into a small military aircraft and took off immediately. Anthony went straight to sleep, and the next thing he knew was Buzz nudging him heavily.

"Whassamatter?" he groaned.

"We've arrived," said Buzz.

Slowly Anthony pulled himself together and, as the aircraft

229

taxied in, he glanced out of the window. They seemed to have landed on the far side of the moon. Outside the window, nothing stretched off forever. Somebody must have made a mistake, decided Anthony. But before he could mention it, Buzz was already unfastening his seat belt and starting to get up. The aircraft stopped and the engine noise died down. Anthony unclipped his own seatbelt and reluctantly followed Buzz up the aircraft to the main door. A gangway had been put in position, and a jeep was waiting at the bottom. As soon as Anthony stepped into the sunlight, he nearly passed out. The heat was unbelievable, and immediately the prickly heat he had developed at Lamboola, started to react. Added to that, the light was blinding, and Anthony found himself tottering down the gangway with his eyes screwed tightly shut. They both climbed into the jeep and it set off straight away, creating a cloud of dust which enveloped them all and, as far as Anthony was concerned, set the seal on the day. He sat with his eyes shut, in abject misery, until the jeep slowed down; then he risked opening them. They had taken a turn round a small fold in the land, and were now driving along a high wire perimeter fence which had been invisible from the airfield. Beyond the fence lay the arsenal which, as far as Anthony could judge at first impression, went on forever. There were low built warehouses laid out in immaculate lines stretching away into the shimmering distance; there were literally thousands of military vehicles, from heavy tanks down to motor-cycles, all parked nose to tail in orderly sections. From the air it must have presented quite a sight; from here on the ground the whole thing just looked too big to comprehend.

They drove along the perimeter wire for a mile until they reached the main gates. There Buzz climbed out of the jeep and, leaving Anthony, went into the guardroom. He came out a minute later and climbed back in. He told the driver where to go, and they were off again, passing through endless lines of armoured cars, tanks, artillery, rocket launchers, jeeps and more tanks. Finally they pulled up outside a group of low buildings and Buzz signalled to Anthony that this was where they got out. A moment later Anthony had passed from the blazing heat of the sun into an air-conditioned atmosphere that threatened to freeze him to death by comparison. Various offices were negotiated, passes were issued, stamped and collected again, finger-prints were taken, as well as full-face photographs; and through all this Anthony moved in a semi-daze, neither knowing nor caring what was happening. Finally he pulled himself together as they were shown into a General's office. The General was a little man, about sixty years old; he was bald, wore rimless spectacles, and his movements were neat and precise. Bird people, thought Anthony; and this impression was confirmed a moment later when the General tweeted at him in a high, reedlike voice.

"Glad to have you with us, Mr. Bridges."

"Thank you, sir. I'm glad to be here," said Anthony, not really quite sure where he was.

"Got a memo from Washington about you. Says I'm to let you have anything you want."

"That's good of them," said Anthony.

"So you just tell me what it is and I'll get working on it. The trains are standing by."

"I don't think I need any trains."

"You need the trains to ship the stuff to the boat," said Buzz, speaking for the first time.

"Oh," said Anthony. "Those trains."

231

"So if you'll just bear with me for one second, we'll get this show on the road," said the General. He pressed a buzzer on his desk and immediately the office became filled with earnest young officers carrying clip-boards and radiating efficiency. "My staff here will make some notes while you talk; that way we'll have everything on record, and you can be away and out of here just as soon as you like." He looked up at the officers who were lined up abreast along the back wall of the office. "Ready, men?"

"Ready, sir," they answered in unison.

"Right, Mr. Bridges, the floor is yours."

Everyone was now looking at Anthony, who realised that he was now supposed to tell them what he wanted. He fumbled in his pocket and finally produced a grubby piece of paper rather like a housewife locating her shopping list in the supermarket.

"Twelve thousand five hundred AR 10s."

"Hawkins!" said the General.

"Twelve thousand five hundred AR 10s. Check, sir," said one of the officers making a note on his clipboard.

"Carry on, Mr. Bridges," said the General.

"Two hundred and fifty light machine-guns," said Anthony, reading from the list.

"What kind?" asked the General.

Anthony looked up at him, surprised. "There's a choice?"

"There certainly is, Mr. Bridges. Hunnaker!" Another officer took a smart pace forward and started spouting names of various types of light machine guns together with their rate of fire, muzzle velocity, calibre and a couple of other technical specifications that Anthony didn't understand either. He sat there until the officer finished and the General looked towards him once more. "Well, Mr. Bridges?"

"Is there anything that you're having particular trouble shifting right now?" asked Anthony, wanting to be helpful.

The General looked towards Hunnaker.

"No, sir. They are all first-class weapons. Perhaps if Mr. Bridges would explain what they're going to be used for?"

"Mr. Bridges?" The General again.

"For killing people, I imagine," said Anthony. He heard something like a snort from Buzz's direction, but it changed into a cough before anyone could really identify it.

"Yes, sir," said Hunnaker. "We realise that. But are the weapons to be used for close field work? Are they to be mobile or permanently sited? Are they to be mounted in weapon carriers, helicopters, motor-cycle side-cars, or are they to be man-handled? What percentage of tracers do you require to each one hundred rounds, and are they going to be used against armour? What are the climatic conditions where the weapons are going to be used and what, if any, are the maintenance facilities? What provisions have been made for training the men who are going to be operating these weapons, and are they required for a two or three-man operation?" Hunnaker paused for breath, and Anthony jumped in quickly.

"I'll leave it entirely up to you," he said.

There was a long silence, eventually broken by Buzz. "He'll take Bartelemess, nine millimetre, all purpose mounting, with ten tracers per hundred, nickel coated."

"Yes, sir," said Hunnaker, stepping back into line.

"All right, Mr. Bridges?" asked the General.

"Sounds first class," said Anthony, with silent thanks to Buzz.

They had the same trouble with the armoured cars and the anti-tank guns. Each time Buzz stepped in at the last moment and trotted out a list of technical specifications which were

233

complete Greek to Anthony, but which seemed to satisfy everyone else. The napalm and the nerve gas also provided a bit of a problem, mainly centering around how the stuff was going to be delivered on to its intended target. As before Anthony had no answer, and Buzz finally settled for five gallon drums of napalm and fifty-pound cylinders of the nerve gas.

"What next, Mr. Bridges?" the General asked, finally.

"Five motor torpedo boats," said Anthony.

"I'll call the Navy," said the General. He made a call to an Admiral, quoted some code words at him, placed his order, and hung up.

"Everything will be at the dock at oh eight-thirty hours tomorrow," he said. "Is there anything else?"

"Perhaps you could tell me where I can find the toilet," said Anthony.

*   *   *

He felt well enough on the flight back to Los Angeles to talk to Buzz Handiman.

"Thanks for taking over back there," he said.

"Self-preservation," said Buzz.

"How do you mean?"

"I'm the one whos going to have to teach those gooks how to use the frigging things."

"You are?"

"Me and my platoon," said Buzz. "We're going with you as weapon advisers."

Anthony thought about this for a few moments. "Isn't that how it started in Vietnam?" he asked finally.

"Sure as hell did."

"I thought so," said Anthony.

*   *   *

Back in Los Angeles it seemed that Buzz had things to do, so Anthony was left to himself for the evening. At seven-thirty he had his dinner sent to his bungalow and at eight-thirty he was sound asleep. The following morning a car picked him up at the hotel at eight a.m. and drove him straight out to the naval dockyard at Long Beach. He was feeling very good this morning. He'd got the arms he needed; Canstartis would be happy, Shirleen would be released, and they would sail off into the sunset together. His euphoria was somewhat shattered though as they drove through the naval dockyard and finally pulled up at his ship's berth. Leaning drunkenly against the side of the quay was the *Maria*.

"With a load like we've got, she'll sink before she leaves the harbour," said Anthony.

"So why did you charter her?" asked Buzz Handiman.

"I didn't."

"I had word that the charter had been arranged by yourself and the CIA," said Buzz.

"They told me they were in the Peace Corps," said Anthony.

"Who did?"

"It doesn't matter," said Anthony. "Have you met the Captain?"

"I have," said Buzz.

"How about the first officer, Mr. Doyle?"

"Him, too."

"Did he . . . ?"

"He did. I broke three of his fingers."

"Oh," said Anthony, feeling slightly sorry for Doyle. "Well, I'd better go and present my compliments to the Captain."

"I've told him we'll be sailing late this afternoon." said Buzz.

Anthony looked around him at the empty quay. "The stuff hasn't even arrived yet," he said.

"It'll be here at oh nine hundred."

"It'll take time to load,"

"This is a naval dockyard," said Buzz. "It'll be loaded."

Happy to leave the responsibility to someone else, Anthony boarded the *Maria*. The bridge was empty, and McGraw was in his cabin, feet up, dressing-gown on. He scowled as Anthony came in.

"Aye," he said. "I thought it might be you."

"Good to see you again Captain," said Anthony. "Congratulations."

"On what?" said McGraw, suspiciously.

"I heard you sold the *Maria*."

"Oh aye. A couple of lunatics in Andestina bought her. Are you acquainted with the large soldier-laddy?"

"Major Handiman? Yes, I know him."

"He'll not be messin' around wi' any of my crew, I trust."

"I doubt it," said Anthony.

"Wha' about his men?"

"What about them?"

"Any homosexuals among 'em?"

"I really don't know."

"Well, we'll see," said McGraw ominously. "Ye'll be takin' your lunch here in my cabin, you and the Major."

Anthony was about to decline, then he decided that he would let Buzz do it. It would mean that they would have to eat at least one meal with the Captain, but it would be worth it just to see how Buzz would deal with the situation of curried haggis with porridge for dessert.

*　　　*　　　*

236

Back on the bridge, Anthony bumped into Doyle, whose left hand was heavily bandaged.

"It's nice to have you aboard again," said Doyle, coyly.

"What happened to your hand?" asked Anthony.

Doyle exposed his badly fitting false teeth. "I caught it in a marine," he said. "My goodness but he's strong."

"Violent, too."

"I know," said the delighted Doyle.

Then a noise on the dockside took Anthony out on to the bridge deck. The train was arriving, and an uncountable number of naval ratings had suddenly appeared on the quay. Portable cranes were being moved into position, and Anthony could see Ram Singh standing next to one of the open holds, arguing vociferously with a large Petty Officer. Eventually Ram Singh gave up and retreated somewhere to sulk, while the Petty Officer started the loading. It was a super-efficient operation, the materials being transferred straight from the flat trucks of the train on to the boat. The train would edge along fifty feet or so, a crane would off-load the truck, transferring the cargo direct to the *Maria*, while the train pulled along another fifty feet, bringing up the next truck in line with the crane. Naval ratings swarmed everywhere, manhandling the small stuff, and working down in the holds. And, as the load was transferred from shore to ship, the *Maria* started to settle lower and lower in the water. After about three hours Anthony found Ram Singh leaning on the forward rail staring morosely over the side.

"We will sink," he said in answer to Anthony's greeting.

"They're sailors," said Anthony. "They know what they're doing."

"Certainly they are sailors, but they are not having to sail aboard the *Maria*."

Anthony leaned over the rail, trying to see what Ram Singh was basing his judgment on.

"See," said Ram Singh. "The Plimsoll line is already below water, and still we are loading."

Anthony glanced over towards the quay. "We're nearly finished," he said.

"As soon as the holds are battened down, they are placing five motor torpedo boats on the deck," said Ram Singh.

Anthony tried to think of something reassuring to say. "Perhaps we'll have fine weather," was all that he could manage.

"If the wind goes higher than a breeze, we will sink like a stone," said Ram Singh. "I think that the time has come for me to sign off from the *Maria*." He turned and walked off in the direction of the bridge. Anthony bumped into him a couple of hours later when the loading had been completed, and they were just about to sail.

"I thought you were leaving," he said.

"The Captain wouldn't pay me," said Ram Singh unhappily. "He owes me for three weeks."

This made Anthony feel a little happier. Any man who was willing to stay aboard for the sake of three weeks' salary couldn't be all that convinced that the ship wasn't going to stay afloat.

*   *   ⊁

Lines were already being cast off when Anthony was called to the main saloon. With Buzz Handiman was a pompous looking State Department official with a vast pile of papers in front of him. As Anthony sat down, the State Department man pushed the papers across the table so that they were in front of him.

"That is a complete inventory of the material that has just

238

been loaded," he said. Then he placed a single sheet of paper on top of the pile. "Sign here please, Mr. Bridges."

"What is it?" said Anthony, taking the proffered pen.

"It is a receipt for the shipment coupled with your personal note setting out the debt."

"What debt?"

"You personally owe the United States Government forty-nine million four hundred and eighty-two thousand, nine hundred and sixty-three dollars and thirty-seven cents."

"The last of the big spenders," said Buzz irreverently, as Anthony signed his name.

Ninety minutes later the tugs gave the *Maria* a final shove towards the open sea, and they were on their way.

* * *

During the voyage, Anthony kept himself pretty much to himself. He had drawn the cabin he had before and he was reasonably content to spend his days therein, dreaming of Shirleen and the wildly erotic times they were going to have together. The business of lunch in the Captain's cabin had been settled first day out. Buzz had taken one mouthful of curried haggis and grown violent. Recognising a formidable adversary when he saw one, the Captain left the field of conflict. Buzz decided that he would spend most of the voyage with the twenty men he had brought with him, and Anthony was left pretty much to his own devices. Whenever he came on deck it was to see Buzz exercising his men, more often than not all twenty of them stark naked. Apart from Doyle, who had somehow had three fingers of his other hand broken, this disturbed no-one. Buzz's platoon were as wicked a looking bunch of characters as Anthony had ever seen. They were all large and hairy, and they all called Buzz and their NCOs

239

by their Christian names. An early dispute with the crew over who slept and ate where had been settled almost immediately, with four of the crew ending up in what passed for the sick bay. With Buzz's men around, Anthony could see there would be no repeat of the last voyage's mutiny.

In spite of Ram Singh's constant predictions otherwise, the *Maria* stayed afloat. She moved pretty sluggishly, but she moved; and McGraw announced on the second day out that with the wind behind them they'd reach Santhoma in a week.

Anthony took to juggling figures to keep himself amused. Canstartis had ordered, and agreed to pay for, fifty million dollars' worth of equipment. Here on board, Anthony had all that he had been asked for, and the price to the Americans was a shade under forty nine and a half million; ergo, half a million dollars for Anthony. The only cloud on the horizon was how he was going to take delivery of the money. He knew that once Canstartis got his hands on the arms, Anthony would die of old age before he saw either money or Shirleen. Therefore a system had to be devised whereby the money was deposited in his Swiss bank before he delivered the consignment. That much he had learned from Walpole. So on the third day out he sent a long cable to Canstartis, giving his estimated date of arrival, and informing the President that he would lay ten miles off shore until payment in Switzerland had been confirmed. Then he would sail into Canstartisville, offload his arms, pick up Shirleen and catch the first plane to civilisation. After that, he would draw a cheque payable to the American Government for forty-nine and a half million dollars; then he would give up work, marry Shirleen and live happily ever after. That was his plan and, as far as he was concerned, the fact that it went hopelessly wrong was nothing to do with him.

10 :::

TO THE DOZEN OR SO PEOPLE IN THE WORLD WHO
knew about it, it was referred to subsequently as the Battle of
Santhoma Sea. Others who knew just that something had
happened but who weren't aware of all of the facts called it
either the South Sea Bubble, or That Monumental Cock Up
Down There. It all started innocently enough on the seventh
morning out. It was a glorious day, the sea as calm and as
beneficent as it had been throughout the voyage. Anthony was
on deck soon after sun-up looking towards the pale smudge of
land that would eventually be their landfall. As he had been
instructed, McGraw had dropped anchor ten miles from
shore. Anthony had sent his arrival cable to Canstartis and

now the whole ship waited for further instructions. The bank in Switzerland was to cable Anthony just as soon as the money had been deposited. With the time differential between Santhoma and Europe, Anthony expected that they would have to spend the best part of the day where they were before they could reasonably expect to hear from Switzerland. He was still leaning on the rail when Buzz Handiman led his men up on deck for the daily bout of calisthenics. Seeing Anthony, Buzz turned his men over to an NCO, and joined him at the rail.

"That it?" he said, nodding towards the distant shoreline.

"That's it," said Anthony.

"Good. The men are getting soft. They need a bit of action."

Anthony glanced over his shoulder to where the marines were thumping up and down on the deck, sweat glistening on their impressive looking bodies.

"They don't look soft to me."

Buzz tapped his forehead with his finger. "Soft up here," he said. "They need to get some killing time in."

Anthony was about to ask what Buzz meant by "killing time" when Buzz interrupted him. "We've got company," he said.

Anthony looked out in the direction that Buzz was staring. About five miles away, heading towards them, was another ship. It was difficult to see exactly what type of ship it was at this distance because the sun was flaring off the water and Anthony had left his sunglasses in his cabin.

"Oh dear!" said Anthony.

"What's wrong?" Buzz asked.

"The last time I was here a boat came to meet us and I sold the consignment to the wrong side." Buzz grunted

242

something unintelligible. Anthony didn't ask him to clarify it because he strongly suspected that it would be uncomplimentary.

Buzz stayed with him a couple more minutes. Until it was confirmed that the ship was definitely heading in their direction; then, without a word, he turned and walked over to the NCO who was drilling the men. He said something to him, the NCO barked out an order, and Buzz's men scampered off below deck. Buzz rejoined Anthony at the rail.

"Won't happen this time," he said laconically.

"What won't?" asked Anthony.

"This time the right side is going to get the stuff."

Five minutes later his men reappeared on deck, wearing their uniforms and armed to the teeth with as impressive an assortment of weapons as Anthony had seen outside a war movie. They ranged from sub-machine guns, through flamethrowers, to a nasty looking bazooka which looked impressive enough to blow a hole in Fort Knox.

"Your men look dangerous," said Anthony nervously.

"That's because they are dangerous," said Buzz.

"Is this just another drill of yours?" asked Anthony hopefully.

"If you give the word that all isn't kosher with this deal, we'll sink that ship in thirty seconds," said Buzz. And Anthony could see no reason to doubt him. The men had looked formidable enough when they were stark naked; now they looked as though they took their orders from Gengis Khan himself.

"I don't know whether violence will solve anything," said Anthony.

"You don't know whether there's anything to solve yet," said Buzz. "But if there is, take my word for it, you'll do a lot better if you clobber them a little." Sinking the ship seemed to be more than "clobbering them a little" and, keeping his fingers crossed, Anthony turned back towards the approaching vessel, hoping sincerely that his growing doubts would turn out to be unfounded.

*   *   *

A shade under half a mile away, the other ship hove to, and they could hear the anchor-chain rattling out across the distance that separated them. She was a freighter, about the same size as the *Maria*, but in much better condition. She was flying a Liberian flag, as was the *Maria*, and with the aid of Buzz's binoculars Anthony made out the name *Katherine* painted on her stern. Also through the binoculars, Anthony could see that the *Maria* was being inspected closely by a small group of men on the *Katherine*'s foredeck. One of them looked vaguely familiar, but even with the aid of the binoculars Anthony was unable to identify him. What could be seen, however, and quite plainly, was the presence of a couple of dozen uniformed and armed men scattered around the deck and superstructure.

"Soldiers," said Anthony. "But they've changed their uniforms since last time I was here."

"Let me see," said Buzz, taking the binoculars. He adjusted them and took a long look. "Commies," he said.

"There aren't any Communists in Santhoma," said Anthony.

"There are now," said Buzz. He handed the binoculars back to Anthony and turned to talk to his NCOs. Anthony had just raised the glasses for another look, when he heard something behind him. He turned round quickly. Buzz's men

244

were clicking in magazines, readying bazooka shells, and uncapping the nozzle of the flame thrower.

"Excuse me," said Anthony. Buzz didn't hear him and he had to repeat himself. "Excuse me," he said, louder this time.

Buzz turned towards him. "What?"

Anthony nodded vaguely towards the marines, who looked as though they were all hanging on a hair trigger. "I mean, isn't this a little bit premature. After all, they're probably the President's men come to welcome us in."

"I told you," said Buzz. "They're Reds."

"But there aren't any Reds in Santhoma. The Communist party is outlawed along with the Conservatives and Socialists. Anyway, how can you tell a man's politics from half a mile away."

"Because the big bastard at the rail over there is wearing the uniform of a major in the Russian army; that's how."

*   *   *

Anthony decided to have another look, centering this time on the small group who were peering towards the *Maria*. His only knowledge of Russian uniforms came from having watched the Red Army choir at the Albert Hall a couple of years back, but he had to admit that the large man with the binoculars, staring straight at him, was wearing a uniform that was strongly reminiscent of the bass baritone's on that occasion. Then he noticed the small man standing next to the officer and obviously talking to him excitedly; and this time he identified him clearly.

"That's Carlos Ramirez," he said to no-one in particular.

"Who's Carlos Ramirez?" asked Buzz.

245

"A friend of mine," said Anthony vaguely, wondering if it were true.

"Sorry about that," said Buzz.

"No reason why you should be," said Anthony. "He's not a bad chap. Rather fun actually."

"I'll tell you what I'll do for you," said Buzz. "I'll give you a chance to get him off the boat."

"What on earth for?" asked Anthony.

"You said he was a friend of yours. I'm giving you a chance to save his life."

"From what?" said the still mystified Anthony.

"Mr. Bridges," said Buzz, using his name for the first time that Anthony could remember. "You are without doubt the most stupid, boneheaded, muscle-brained prick that I have ever encountered. You haven't the beginning of an idea which end is up; you start fights in bars without being able to handle them; you can't hold your liquor; you don't know the barrel of a gun from your own asshole; you're so full of limey shit that it's coming out of your ears; you have the imagination of a cretin; the physique of a faggot; and the mentality of a Boy Scout. Now hear this, Mister. You have fifteen minutes to get your friend off that ship before I sink it and every Commie rat on board."

"I say," said Anthony, more surprised than anything else. "That's a bit strong, isn't it?"

"So what?"

"But it's an unarmed merchant vessel."

"So are we," said Buzz.

Anthony glanced at Buzz's men, bristling with firepower. "But they're flying a Liberian flag. That makes them Liberians," he said.

"So are we."

246

"It'll cause an international incident."

"One Liberian ship sinking another; there ain't nothing international about that."

"I don't think it's a very good idea," said Anthony.

Buzz shoved his face to within two inches of Anthony, who noticed that the marine major's mouth had started to fleck with foam at the corners. He's a raving nut, thought Anthony. "Listen you cocksuckingmotherfucker," said Buzz. "I've put up with your limey crap for two weeks now. This is the end of the line. From hereonin I take over, me and Uncle Sam, whom I represent. On that ship over there are Russians and just everyone knows that the Russians are the enemy. Do you understand that? The enemy! And when I come across the enemy, I kill 'em because, sure as God made little green apples, that's the only way we're going to get peace in this world. Right?"

Anthony didn't reply; he was watching in horrified fascination as Buzz worked himself up into paranoia and beyond.

"Now like I said," Buzz went on. "You've got fifteen minutes to get your friend off that ship, starting from now." He turned and stalked off, stiff-legged, like some mechanical robot that had just been re-programmed as a killing machine.

Anthony stood where he was for a moment wondering what the hell to do next. Then he had an idea. If he could talk to Carlos and get him to persuade the Russians to back off a few miles, then Buzz wouldn't be able to do anything to them; certainly the *Maria* wasn't equipped to give chase. He turned to Ram Singh, who had been watching for the past five minutes with morbid disinterest. "Lower me a boat," he said. Ram Singh looked at him blankly and very conscious of the occasion Anthony lost his temper for the first time that he could remember. "Get on with it, you idle wog! Move yourself and lower me a boat!"

Ram Singh drew himself up proudly. "You are not calling me a wog," he said. "I am a Sikh."

"If you don't lower me a boat," said Anthony. "I'll tell the Captain you've been sleeping with the entire crew for the past six months."

Ram Singh went a little pale. "It's not true," he said.

"By the time you convince him of that, he'll have thrown you overboard. Now lower me a boat."

"Yes, sir," said Ram Singh, and started shouting orders to the crew.

Anthony looked across towards the *Katherine* again. There was some activity on her deck now but, without binoculars, Anthony couldn't make it out, and he didn't feel inclined to ask Buzz for a loan of his. Two minutes later his boat had been swung out. Anthony clambered in and told Ram Singh to start lowering. His head was just sinking below the level of the deck when he heard a shout from the bridge.

"Where d'ye think you're makin' off wi' one of my lifeboats?" yelled McGraw. "Put it back where it belongs this instant, d'ye hear me."

The men on the winches hestitated and Ram Singh looked towards the bridge, and then back at Anthony, trying to gauge the lesser of two evils. At that moment Buzz came over to the rail and looked down at Anthony. He had put on a steel helmet, strapping it under his chin, and he was nursing a sub-machine gun and bristling with knives and small arms and grenades; he was a personification of every anti-war cartoon that had ever been drawn. "You've got ten minutes left," he said.

Anthony, who was beginning to panic, decided that if Buzz

248

was as capable of scaring him as he was, perhaps he would have the same effect on McGraw.

"Tell the Captain to let me take his lifeboat then," he said.

At that moment McGraw yelled out again, this time direct to Ram Singh. "Reel that boat in, ye heathen wog or I'll throw ye overboard."

Buzz looked up towards the bridge and shouted at McGraw. "Shut your fat mouth, Captain. I'm in charge now." Then to Ram Singh, "Now lower away, you stupid coon, or I'll cut your nuts off." A nervous wreck by now, Ram Singh gave the order to continue lowering and then, as a small gesture of defiance, he cut loose the boat while she was still six feet above sea level.

The boat hit the water with a crash that threatened to take the bottom right out of her. But she remained afloat, and by the time Anthony had picked himself up from the bottom, she had drifted a few yards from the *Maria*. Anthony had always thought of the *Maria* as a small vessel, but from his present viewpoint, she looked immense. He shipped a couple of oars, wondering why he hadn't commandeered a couple of the crew to do the heavy work; but there wasn't time to do anything about it now, and he started rowing as hard as he could towards the *Katherine*. His back was towards her, so he didn't see that she, too, had lowered a boat. In it was one man, and he was rowing towards the *Maria*. It was Carlos Ramirez.

"Old, old friend," he said, as the boats bumped into one another.

"Hello, Carlos," said Anthony.

Then they both spoke at the same time. "You have five minutes to get aboard the *Maria/Katherine* before the *Katherine/Maria* is sunk."

And, having spoken, they spent the next fifteen seconds staring at one another, trying to work out what the other had said. Then, simultaneously, they both looked towards the ships, then back at one another.

"Is using your boat or mine?" asked Carlos.

"Yours," said Anthony. "It looks safer."

He clambered into Carlos' boat, took one of the oars and they both started rowing hard. They just managed to clear the centre line between the two ships when it all started.

*　　　*　　　*

Subsequently they argued as to who had fired the first shot, but they never did get to agree. It didn't really matter, because as soon as one fired the other was firing back like there was no tomorrow. And for the *Maria* and *Katherine* and most of the personnel on board, there wasn't. It was small arms first, which rattled against the sides of each ship. Buzz's flame-thrower proved ineffective because the range was too great; all it did was to set light to a patch of sea which threatened to burn up Anthony and Carlos. They continued to row hard as both Buzz and his opposite number on the *Katherine* decided to use the heavy stuff. Buzz had a bazooka, the Russians a ten-inch mortar. After a couple of misses, the bazooka blew a hole in the side of the *Katherine* at almost the same moment as the mortar dropped a shell down the smoke stack of the *Maria*.

The *Maria* went off more spectacularly as the mortar blew her bottom out and her top off simultaneously. The *Katherine* looked as though she were going to last a little longer; then a blazing chunk of *Maria* drove straight through the hole made by the bazooka shell and landed in a hold crammed with forty million dollars' worth of Russian arms and ammunition. Anthony and Carlos were just picking themselves up from the bottom of the lifeboat, having been knocked there by the explosion of the *Maria*, when the *Katherine* went up likewise, and they were back in the bottom of the boat again while bullets and shells whizzed and hummed all around them. Two minutes later, when the racket had died down, they risked a look. There were two patches of oily water and assorted floating debris. Nothing else at all, save for an acrid pall of smoke as a marker.

*   *   *

"I told him not to do it," said Anthony.

"Me, I am telling the Major Karkov the same thing," said Carlos.

They were sitting in the stern of the lifeboat sharing a bottle of rum from the emergency rations they had found. It was a couple of hours later and they had drifted well out to sea in a medium offshore breeze that had sprung up. Their decision not to go in towards Santhoma had been unanimous; there could be nothing but trouble for them there. There was plenty of food and water in the lifeboat, so they decided to drift awhile. Then, after finishing the bottle of rum, they would make up their minds in which direction to head.

"How did you get into this, ol' pal?" asked Anthony.

"I am hearing that you are getting arms for Canstartis from the Americans; so I am guessing that the Russians will be wanting to give arms to Dolivera. They are very clever, the Russians, and they are needing a middle man I am thinking. I, Carlos Santos Miguel Anthonio Ramirez, am becoming their middle man."

251

"Well done, ol' buddy," said Anthony, passing him the bottle.

There was a few minutes' silence while they each took another drink.

"I owe the American Government forty-nine and a half million dollars," said Anthony, after a while.

"I am owing the Russians thirty-nine and three quarter million dollars," said Carlos. "In roubles."

"In roubles?" said Anthony. "That's interesting."

"Have another drink," said Carlos.

"Thank you," said Anthony.

*　　　*　　　*

Two hours later they both stood in the lifeboat, their arms around each other for support, while they waved and shouted towards a small freighter which was heading across their path. Somebody on board must have spotted them, because the freighter changed course slightly and headed towards them.

"We're saved, ol' friend," said Anthony, with a sob in his voice.

"Snitched from the jawbone of the sea," said Carlos, tears streaming down his face.

They were still standing in the lifeboat, waving, five minutes later when the freighter tried to ram them.

*　　　*　　　*

"The bloody boat was full of Chinese," said Anthony, when he had dragged himself back into the swamped lifeboat once more. He vividly recalled a row of impassive Oriental faces staring down at him from the ship's rail as she had missed them by inches and swept past, bumping the

252

lifeboat along her hull, threatening to overturn her at any second.

"I am not seeing Chinese," said Carlos. "I am only seeing General Guardino."

They both stopped baling and looking out towards the ship, moving away from them fast, heading towards Santhoma.

"There'll be a change of Government there tomorrow," said Anthony.

"*Sí*," said Carlos. "Canstartis has no guns. Dolivera has no guns. *Viva Presidente Guardino.*"

"Poor Shirleen," said Anthony.

*   *   *

They were picked up two days later by a Panamanian freighter heading towards her home port and after twenty-four hours they landed in Panama. Having no passports looked as though it might turn out to be a problem, but Carlos produced a second cousin who worked for the Government, and everything was arranged smoothly. There was the question of payment and, having no money, Anthony was forced to use one of his credit cards to raise the necessary entrance fee, hoping that word hadn't leaked out that the card had been cancelled. And, having used the card once and got away with it, he and Carlos moved into the best hotel in town.

*   *   *

"What are your plans, old friend?" Carlos asked Anthony at dinner that night.

"I was going to marry Miss Jones, but she's probably been executed by now."

"Such a terrible waste," sighed Carlos.

253

"So I'll just go home, I suppose."

"How are you going to get home? You have no passport."

Anthony thought about this for a moment. "I suppose your second cousin . . . ?"

Carlos shook his head. "I fear not, old friend. However, I have another cousin . . ."

Carlos' other cousin headed up the local branch of the Mafia. Not much happened in Panama, so it was only a small branch, but their contacts were good and a British passport could be purchased for two thousand seven hundred dollars.

"Can I sign for it on my Diners Card?" asked Anthony.

Carlos shook his head. "But you have two thousand seven hundred dollars in Switzerland," he said. "Your commission on your first deal." Anthony had forgotten about this, and was a little surprised that Carlos hadn't also. "You sign the money over to me," continued Carlos. "And I will arrange to get it to my cousin in the Mafia."

"I'll need something for my aeroplane ticket," said Anthony.

Carlos spread his hands widely. "Your ticket is included of course," he said generously.

"How long will it take?"

"Two days," said Carlos. "In three days you can be back in your wonderful city of London."

*   *   *

And so it was. Three days later Anthony landed at London Airport in the middle of a snowstorm. He called a friend from the airport, who offered to give him a bed for a couple of nights, and then took the airport bus to the West London terminal. At the terminal he bought an evening paper. Buried away on page eight was a small, single column story from the

254

paper's South American bureau. It seemed that there had been an armed uprising in Santhoma, and the new President was one General Guardino. One of his first official acts had been to sign death warrants for twenty Red Chinese nationals who had somehow managed to sneak into the country. His second official act had been to announce his forthcoming marriage to a Miss Shirleen Jones.

*   *   *

Anthony was at a party in the King's Road. It was a dull party, and the girl he had come with was even duller. After an hour, he found himself in a corner with a girl he hadn't met before. They introduced themselves and started talking inconsequentials. Ten minutes later, his host of the past couple of days sidled up to him.

"Have to find yourself another pad tonight," he said. "I've got something good going for me." And he sidled away again before Anthony could comment.

"I've got a spare bed," said his new companion.

"What does your father do for a living?" asked Anthony.

"He's a wholesale greengrocer."

Anthony thought about this for a moment. "Ta," he said; and that was that.